THE CURSE OF THE
CAMPFIRE
WEENIES

AND OTHER WARPED AND CREEPY TALES

STARSCAPE BOOKS BY DAVID LUBAR

Novels

Flip

Hidden Talents

True Talents

Story Collections

*In the Land of the Lawn Weenies
and Other Warped and Creepy Tales*

*Invasion of the Road Weenies
and Other Warped and Creepy Tales*

THE CURSE OF THE CAMPFIRE WEENIES

AND OTHER WARPED AND CREEPY TALES

DAVID LUBAR

STARSCAPE

A TOM DOHERTY ASSOCIATES BOOK
NEW YORK

This is a work of fiction. All of the characters, organizations, and events portrayed in this novel are either products of the author's imagination or are used fictitiously.

THE CURSE OF THE CAMPFIRE WEENIES AND OTHER WARPED AND CREEPY TALES

Copyright © 2007 by David Lubar
Reader's Guide copyright © 2008 by Tor Books

"Head of the Class" originally appeared in *Boy's Life*, October 2004.
"Picking Up" originally appeared in *Boy's Life*, May 2004.

All rights reserved.

A Starscape Book
Published by Tom Doherty Associates, LLC
175 Fifth Avenue
New York, NY 10010

www.tor-forge.com

ISBN-13: 978-0-7653-5771-7
ISBN-10: 0-7653-5771-2

First Edition: September 2007
First Mass Market Edition: December 2007
Second Mass Market Edition: August 2008

Printed in the United States of America

0 9 8 7 6 5 4 3 2 1

For Matthew, Doris, Caroline,
and Shannon Tyburczy.
Thanks for all the good times,
cold drinks, and burned hot dogs.

CONTENTS

CONTENTS

THE CURSE OF THE

CAMPFIRE

WEENIES

AND OTHER WARPED AND CREEPY TALES

MR. HOOHAA!

I can stare a werewolf in the face and laugh. I can step up to a vampire and shake his cold, undead hand without trembling. No problem. I've sat through every horror movie that's ever come to our town and visited dozens of Halloween haunted houses. Monsters don't even make me twitch. But clowns creep me out big-time.

That usually isn't a problem. I mean, most days, you just aren't going to run into a guy with a round red nose, a huge painted smile, and wild green hair unless you live in a circus town or something. But my little brother's birthday was coming up, and Benji was determined to have a clown.

"That's a waste of money," I told my mom. "I can entertain the kids." How hard could it be to keep a bunch of six-year-olds amused? I could just push my palm against my mouth and make fart sounds. That alone would keep them happy for at least fifteen minutes.

"It's nice you want to help, Andrew," my mom said.

"But Benji has his heart set on a clown. And I found this ad in the paper." She held up the local weekly. There was a small ad that just read: "Mr. HooHaa! The perfect clown for parties."

"Looks kind of cheesy," I said.

But Mom wouldn't listen. She made the call and booked Mr. HooHaa! for Benji's party.

"You don't need me, then, right?" I asked after she'd hung up.

"Of course I'll need you," she said.

"But . . ."

"And Benji will want you there."

So, two weeks later, I found myself filling bowls with potato chips, lining up plastic cups, and helping Mom string streamers and balloons in the living room.

About fifteen minutes after the brats—I mean guests—arrived, I glanced out the window just as a van pulled up to the curb. The van was white, with a big smile painted on the side. Above the smile was the name "Mr. HooHaa!"

"Everything's set," I said to Mom. "Can I go hang out with my friends now?"

"You can't leave," she said. "You'll miss the clown."

That's my plan.

The doorbell rang.

"Would you get that?" she asked.

I tried to think of an excuse. The bell rang again.

One of the kids screamed as he spilled half a cup of purple juice on his shirt. Two other kids dumped their juice on him. Mom dashed over, then glanced back at me and said, "Get the door, please." She turned to the kids and said, "The clown is here."

As shouts of "Yay!" filled the air, I headed for the door. I really didn't want to open it, but I guess I had no choice. *It won't be that bad*, I told myself. I was wrong. He was standing on the porch. A clown. A creepy, spooky, shivery clown, who smelled like medicine and mildew. I couldn't pick out any one part of him that, by itself, was scary, but the sight of him still made me shudder.

I opened the door wider and stepped aside, so I could stay as far away from him as possible. He walked in, pointed a squeeze horn at me, and honked it a couple times. *Wonka-wonka.*

"This way," I said, heading for the living room.

He rushed past me, leaped into the room, and shouted, "Hey, boys and girls, it's HooHaa! time!" Even his voice made me cringe.

I wasn't alone. Half the kids started crying. One tried to crawl under the couch, and another curled into such a tight ball, I was afraid he'd disappear. The clown ignored them and started pulling this really long handkerchief out of his sleeve. Then he honked his horn and fell down. Mom ran around, soothing freaked-out tykes. Benji seemed okay, so I slunk from the room, shivering all the way down to my bones and back up to my clammy flesh.

This is so stupid, I told myself. It was ridiculous to be afraid of some guy with a painted face and big shoes. I stepped outside to get away from the laughs and cries.

"Grow up," I muttered, hating myself for acting like

one of Benji's friends. I stared at the van. Even with the clown smile painted on its side, it wasn't scary. I liked cars and trucks. I understood how they worked and how they were made. I wandered over and looked inside. The back-seats had been removed. There was a table there, with a mirror on it. I guess he did his makeup in the van.

I looked back at the house. Then I looked in the van again and stared at the mirror. Maybe there was a way to get over my fear.

I remembered last year, when Benji had been scared by the vacuum cleaner. I could have told him to stop acting like a baby, but I knew that wouldn't help. Instead, I'd unplugged the vacuum, opened it up, and showed him how it worked. Knowledge beats fear, every time.

I went back inside and waited. Mom had only hired Mr. HooHaa! for an hour. Right after he left and I'd heard the van door close, I slipped back outside. I snuck over to the window, hoping he'd take off his makeup before he drove away.

It was that simple. If I saw him go from clown to man, maybe that would get rid of my fear. I peeked inside. Yes. He was sitting at the table. I watched him reach up and pull off the rubber nose.

I let out a gasp as his real nose unrolled. It was thin and long, like a tiny flattened elephant's trunk that dangled just past his chin. He stripped off his wig, revealing a brain covered by a transparent membrane webbed with tiny veins. Then he reached toward his mouth. As he peeled off the huge red lips, I realized they weren't painted on. They were plastic. They'd concealed a gumless cluster of long brown teeth that jutted from his jaw like stalactites. He pulled off the gloves. His fingers seemed boneless, like bloated worms. As he leaned over to remove his shoes, I was thankful I couldn't see what was really at the end of his legs.

I ducked down as he got up from his seat. A moment later, the van started and Mr. HooHaa! pulled away from the curb. As the van made a left turn at the end of the block, I saw the driver's window roll down. A horn stuck out, clutched in those wormlike fingers. He squeezed a short double honk into the air, then drove out of sight.

I stood there for a long time, trying to convince myself I'd been mistaken or fooled in some way. I wanted to believe I hadn't really seen the things I'd just witnessed. But it was all real. Beneath his makeup, this clown was far worse than anything I could have imagined.

I sighed and headed inside. As soon as I stepped through the doorway, Benji ran up to me and hugged my leg. "I don't think I like clowns anymore," he said. "They're sort of scary."

"You got that right." I picked him up and carried him on my shoulders back to the party. "No more clowns."

"But I'm a big boy," he said. "Big boys don't get scared."

"Sure we do." I lifted him off my shoulders and deposited him in the midst of his cake-stuffed, sugar-cranked friends. "We just learn to hide it."

I was more afraid of clowns than ever. But I guess, in a way, that wasn't such a bad thing. Until today, I had been afraid of them for no reason. Now, it was no longer a silly fear. I wonder whether that will make it any easier to hide.

YOU ARE WHAT
YOU EAT

Dale flashed me an evil grin as he held up the jar. "I'll give you a buck to eat it."

"It's probably spoiled," I said. We were down in his basement, surrounded by stacks of boxes and piles of magazines. As far as I could see, his folks had never thrown anything out.

"Okay, then. Two bucks." He put his hand on the lid of the jar.

"The whole thing?" I asked.

He pointed at the bottom of the label. "It's only a couple ounces."

I gave the offer serious thought as I looked at the shelves. There must have been hundreds of cans and jars. The stuff ranged from pickles, to soup, to nuts. And to what Dale had in his hand. Baby food. Since Dale was the youngest kid in his family and since he hadn't been a baby for a long time, the food had to be at least ten or twelve years old.

"Five bucks," Dale said. "That's my last offer."

"Deal." Hey, five bucks is five bucks. I took the jar and untwisted the lid. It made that hissing, vacuum sound, which was a good sign. I stuck two fingers in the goop—the label said "strained peaches"—and scooped up a big glob.

It didn't taste bad. In either sense of the word. I got the rest of the glop from the jar, licked my fingers, then held out my hand for my money. "Pay up."

That's when my legs wobbled. *Uh-oh.* . . .

I took a step back, staggered another step, lost my ability to stand, and plopped down on my butt. I looked up at Dale. Way up. He was huge.

Dale stared back down at me from far away. His expression was weird—like he couldn't believe his eyes.

"What's wrong?" I asked. At least, that's what I planned to ask. But my lips and tongue turned it into, "Wuhhba wummm?"

"You're a baby," Dale said.

"And you're a jerk." That sentence didn't come out any clearer than the other one. I tried to stand. And discovered I couldn't make my body do what I wanted. I looked at my legs. They'd disappeared into my pants. I looked at my arms. I could barely see the tips of pudgy little fingers sticking out of my sleeves. My shirt was huge.

No. My shirt was fine.

I was a baby. Because I'd eaten baby food. I waited for Dale to get help. Instead, he turned to the shelves, said,

"Cool," and started searching through the cans and jars. "What else can we turn you into?"

"Stop fooling around!" As I screamed at Dale, I realized I didn't have any teeth. That was such a shock, it was a moment before I realized something even worse. A feeling of warmth in the vicinity of my lap drove home the fact that I lacked control over my body functions. I hoped Dale wouldn't notice. No such luck.

"Oh, that's just gross," he said. "I'll get a mop. But you're cleaning it up."

Right. Like I could handle a mop. He walked past me. I heard him go upstairs. Desperately, I scanned the shelves for something that could make me a boy again. Boysenberry jelly? No, too much of a stretch. Kidney beans? Too risky. I wanted to be a kid, not a kidney.

Manwich!

That's as close as I was going to get. It was on the second shelf. I rolled over, then grabbed the shelf and pulled myself to my feet. I could barely stand. I braced myself with my elbows and picked up the can.

It had a pull-top lid. I yanked at it, but there was no way I could budge it.

I heard Dale heading back.

I put the can on its side, grabbed the pull tab with both hands, and let myself fall. I landed hard on my back. The lid pulled free. Manwich plopped out of the can. I opened my mouth as it rained on my face. I swallowed. Yum. Even cold, it was pretty tasty.

"What's going on?" Dale asked.

He stood there with a mop in his hand, looking up at me.

I had to admit, I enjoyed looking down at him.

"I had a snack while you were gone." I pointed to the rest of the spilled can. "Looks like you've got a lot of cleaning up to do."

Dale started to open his mouth, but I guess he realized he had to do whatever I told him. I could get used to being a man.

As he mopped the floor, I searched through a stack of boxes until I found clean clothes that fit me. Then I looked through the shelves some more. I figured that after he'd finished mopping and after he'd paid me my five dollars I was going to reward Dale with a snack. Something interesting. Cat food would work. Or more baby food. I wondered whether his folks had any goat cheese in the fridge upstairs?

*SPIN

Jimmy was only five, but he could spin things. Balls, toys, dishes—if it could rotate at all, Jimmy would spin it. This drove his brother, Darrin, crazy. Jimmy didn't care. Darrin could shout and stomp around all day. It didn't matter. As long as there was something to spin, Jimmy hardly noticed anything else.

At the moment, he was sitting in the living room, spinning a book on his finger. It was a small book, but that was because Jimmy had small fingers.

"Stop it," Darrin snarled.

Jimmy ignored him.

"Get out of here. I'm trying to watch TV," Darrin said.

Jimmy spun the book in the other direction.

Darrin threw down the remote control. "Mom," he called, "I'm going out."

"Take your brother."

"No!"

"Then you can stay home."

"Oh, all right." Darrin grabbed Jimmy's arm, yanking hard enough so the book went flying.

Jimmy let himself get dragged along. He was happy. There were lots of things to spin outside.

Darrin stopped at his friend Ray's house.

"Why you got him?" Ray asked, pointing at Jimmy.

"Mom made me. Come on. Let's go to the playground."

Ray came out, carrying a basketball. Jimmy reached for it. Ray leaned down and started to hand the ball to Jimmy, then snatched it back and laughed. "Sucker."

Jimmy didn't cry. He was pretty sure there'd be something to spin at the playground.

When they got there, Darrin and Ray shot baskets. Jimmy knew he couldn't have the ball while they were playing. He looked around for something else and found an empty soda can. He spun it on the hard, black asphalt. It made a wonderful sound.

Darrin rushed over to him. "Don't play with garbage!" He kicked the can, sending it flying across the basketball court. Then he turned to Ray. "Come on. Let's go to the swings."

Jimmy watched the two of them walk into the sandy area with the swings, slide, and climbing fort. Ray put the basketball down and got on a swing.

Jimmy walked over toward the ball. "Touch it and you're dead," Ray said.

Jimmy looked at his big brother. But Darrin didn't help him. Jimmy wandered around the edge of the play area, searching for something to spin. He found a paper plate. There was a thin string of pizza cheese sticking to it, but he didn't care.

"For crying out loud!" Darrin screamed as Jimmy spun the plate. "Will you stop with the garbage?" He jumped off the swing, grabbed Jimmy, and dragged him across the sand.

Jimmy struggled to get free. "Give me a hand," Darrin shouted.

Ray came over and grabbed Jimmy's legs. The two of them carried Jimmy to the other side of the play area and plunked him on the highest platform of the climbing fort. "Stay there."

As Darrin and Ray walked back toward the swings, Jimmy started to climb down.

Darrin spun back and screamed at him, "You stay right there! Don't you dare move."

Jimmy stayed. He looked for something to spin. There didn't seem to be anything he could reach. And Darrin would get angry if he tried to climb down. Then he noticed some sand on the platform. Jimmy dropped one tiny grain onto his palm. It was too small to spin like a ball or a book, but there were other ways.

"Spin," he whispered.

The grain spun in his palm. It tickled a little. Jimmy liked that. He made more sand spin.

All around, the sand spun. It didn't spin in a whirl, like a tornado. Each grain spun by itself. The sand on the bottoms of Jimmy's sneakers spun, making the rubber heat up and smoke. Jimmy didn't mind. There wasn't a whole lot of sand on his sneakers.

Down below, there was a lot of sand. Darrin and Ray, caught between the fort and the swings, froze as the sand etched away the soles of their sneakers. By the time they realized they needed to run, they couldn't.

Jimmy kept spinning the sand. He heard some screams, but they didn't last very long, and he didn't pay any attention to them. He was used to getting screamed at.

When he was tired and ready to go home, he looked around for his brother. But there wasn't any sign of Darrin or Ray. That was okay. Darrin was always running off without him. Jimmy could climb down by himself. And he knew how to get home. Maybe he'd even find something interesting to spin on the way.

THE TUNNEL OF TERROR

No way," Rachel said. "You guys go. I'll wait out here." She put her hand on the sun-heated railing outside the entrance to the Tunnel of Terror ride.

"Come on," Penny said. "It'll be fun. And we already went on the rides that you wanted."

"Yeah," Trish said, rubbing her shoulder. "We did those stupid bumper cars twice. I don't even like them. Come on. Let's have some real fun."

"It can't be that scary," Penny said.

Rachel looked at the ride. Each car rolled along a short entryway, pushed through double doors, vanished inside a shabby wooden building, then eventually emerged from another set of doors at the far end of the loading platform.

It'll be dark in there, she thought. But it was the middle of the day. The sun was high. Rachel figured there would be some cracks of light seeping in. And she could always close her eyes. She took a deep breath. Then, as the air flowed from her lungs, she managed to say, "Okay."

"Super." Penny rushed around the railing.

"Great." Trish grabbed Rachel's arm and ran toward the entrance.

"Is it scary?" Rachel asked as she gave her ticket to the old man who was sitting on a stool by the gate.

The man shrugged. "That's up to you." He tore her ticket in half and dropped the pieces in a plastic bucket. "But we always give you what you pay for."

Before Rachel could ask what he meant, she was herded to the loading area by her friends. As the first car stopped, Penny and Trish jumped in. Rachel realized the car was too small for three riders.

"Hey!" she called, but the car rolled away. Rachel didn't want to get too far behind her friends. She jumped into the next car, all by herself, and pulled down the safety bar.

"It won't be bad," she said, speaking aloud to bolster her courage. She kept up the pep talk in her mind: *It's just going to be some mechanical monsters or some stuff painted on the walls. Maybe some dummies with fake blood.*

The car moved toward the double doors. In the dim light, Rachel could see brushstrokes in the flat black paint. Ahead, Penny and Trish's car pushed open the doors, then slipped inside. The tall back of the car hid them from Rachel's view.

Here goes, Rachel thought, as her own car reached the doors and pushed them open with a thud, jolting her against the bar.

When the doors slammed shut behind her, Rachel

entered a darkness so deep it was as if the world had never known such a thing as vision. The room was beyond blackness, a cave within a cave wrapped in layers of velvet.

Only the jostling of the car let Rachel know she was moving.

"Penny?" she called out, listening for the sound of another car or the giggles of her friends. "Trish?"

Her words seemed unable to travel through the darkness. She heard no answer.

The car spun suddenly, turning sharply to the left and shooting forward. Rachel screamed as she found herself face-to-face with a grinning skull. The jaws of the skull gaped wide, then snapped shut. Rachel grabbed the safety bar to keep from leaping out of her seat.

Before her scream ended, the car spun away with another jolting twist, leaving the image of the skull burned in her vision as the blackness returned.

Calm down, she told herself. *It's make-believe.* She felt foolish for screaming. All she'd seen was a piece of plastic shaped like a bone. Nothing real. No true terrors.

The car lurched again.

A man rose up with an ax in his hands. One of his eyes dangled from its socket.

Another scream burst from Rachel's lungs. The car spun back into blackness, then shot almost instantly toward a chamber where a hand thrust up from a freshly dug grave.

Rachel squeezed her eyes shut. She gripped the bar with both hands and thought about running from the car.

Even in her panic, she understood that this would be too dangerous.

"I'll wait," she said out loud. "I'll just wait until it's over." She knew she could survive the ride if she kept her eyes closed.

The car lurched. Through shut lids Rachel sensed a flash of brightness. She pulled one hand from the bar and covered her eyes, trying to screen out even the faintest hint of what lay in front of her.

Something brushed her cheek and the back of her hand.

String, she thought as a small shriek escaped her lips. That's all it was. Dangling pieces of string.

Another lurch . . .

Leading to another flash.

And another.

Soon, Rachel thought. *Not much longer.* It was a cheap ride in a cheap amusement park. There was no way the ride would last much longer.

It didn't.

A few more lurches and she felt a bump as the car pushed through another pair of swinging doors.

Rachel quickly dropped her hand and opened her eyes. Bright light made her blink. She stumbled off the car and walked to the exit gate, where her friends were waiting.

"Cool," Penny said.

"Kinda hokey," Trish said. She looked at Rachel. "Well? What'd you think?"

Rachel shrugged. "It was okay."

"Not too scary for you?" Penny asked.

"Not at all." As Rachel walked along the railing, the ticket man smiled at her. Then he squeezed both eyes shut and curled his lips in mock terror.

Rachel turned away from him. *He knows*, she thought. But that didn't matter. It was over and done with.

"Come on," Rachel said, tapping Penny on the shoulder. "How about the bumper cars again? What do you—"

The words froze in Rachel's mouth as Penny glanced back toward her. Penny's flesh had turned ancient and wrinkled. Her teeth were yellow and broken, her hair nothing more than wispy strands of white stitched to her scalp. Rachel gasped and closed her eyes. When she opened them, everything was normal.

"What?" Penny asked. "Is something wrong?"

"No." Rachel shook her head. She looked away. *It's my imagination*, she thought. *The ride just made me imagine that.* She stared at a tree across the path.

A man was impaled on one of the branches, pierced right below his chest. He hung limp and dead. A buzzard sat on his shoulder, pecking at his face.

Rachel gasped and pointed. She looked toward her friends, then back at the tree.

The image vanished. In her head, Rachel heard the words of the ticket man: *We always give you what you pay for.*

Rachel realized she was still pointing. Her own hand had turned to fleshless bone.

She thrust it from her sight and looked toward the ground.

A screaming face rose from the earth at her feet. Rachel lifted her gaze toward the sky. The clouds became severed heads, bloated and bleached white as if they'd been submerged in saltwater for days.

Rachel stared straight ahead, afraid to shut her eyes again, afraid that any attempt to escape from the images would bring something even worse. As she rushed to catch up with her friends, she wondered how much longer the ride would last.

A NICE CLEAN PLACE

The west side of Gunderson Park is pretty dirty and disgusting. I'm not one of those prissy girls who're scared of a little mud or grease, but the place is bad enough to make me shudder. There's the trash, of course—candy wrappers, plastic bags, and just about everything else people might throw away. But the place is also loaded with pigeons. And everyone knows what pigeons are loaded with. The statue of General Treron at the far corner of the park is so thick with pigeon droppings you could probably jab a finger into it halfway to the first knuckle without hitting stone.

I wouldn't ever choose to be anywhere around there, except it's a good shortcut to get from town to my street without passing those creepy boys who hang out by the magazine shop. Normally, I'd walk in front of the statue, but I saw Monica Entermayer heading in my direction and I really didn't want to get trapped into listening to her brag some more about her trip to France. So I ducked in back of General Treron.

That's how I ended up stepping into a hole behind the statue and falling down into Zupthweld. Luckily, I landed on a bush. Still, I was kind of shaken and just stayed there, feeling totally confused.

"Hello, Topsider. Welcome to Zupthweld. I am Hobart."

I stared up at the man who was greeting me. Except for his extremely pasty complexion, he looked like any other adult. "Hi," I said. "I'm Steffie."

He extended a hand to help me climb out of the bush. "It has been many years since we last had a visitor. I'd be proud to show you the fine points of our marvelous city before you return to Topside."

"Thanks." I noticed I was at the top of a steep hill. A large town was spread out below. Far into the distance I saw houses with neat lawns laid out on wide, clean streets.

"This way," Hobart said.

I followed along as he pointed out the features of Zupthweld. There was a school and a ballpark and lots of houses and some factories. It wasn't much different from Topside—I mean from home—except that it was amazingly clean. The people we met all smiled at me. Everyone was happy and friendly.

"Well," Hobart said as we returned to the bush on the hilltop where I'd fallen. "I guess that's the end of the tour. Let me help you back to Topside. I'll fetch a ladder."

"Great." I looked up at the hole I'd fallen through. "Hey, before I go, there's one thing I have to know."

"Yes?"

"How do you keep it so clean?" I asked.

Hobart chuckled. "The founder of Zupthweld, who lived many, many years ago, was a great inventor. And this was his greatest invention. Observe." With that, Hobart reached into his pocket and took out a stick of gum. He put the gum in his mouth but tossed the wrapper on the ground.

There was an immediate flutter of wings. A pigeon dove on the trash and ate it. The bird just swallowed down the wrapper like it was a tasty treat. I watched, following the upward path as the bird flew out the hole that led to Topside.

"You get rid of all your garbage that way?" I asked.

Hobart grinned. "Indeed. It's a perfect system—a triumph of biomechanical engineering. They process all our waste and dispose of it. Now stay right here. I'll be back in a moment."

I waited while he dashed off. He returned with a long ladder. "Thanks for the tour," I said. "It's a nice town." I climbed the ladder and squeezed through the hole, back to the filthy mess of the west side of the park.

Right behind me, several pigeons fluttered out. They bombed the statue, adding to the layer on General Treron's left shoulder, then dove back into the hole—obviously in search of more garbage. I thought about the clean streets of Zupthweld and where all their trash ended up.

"Our turn," I said, looking around for what I needed. I found a large rock, big enough to cover the hole but not so big that I couldn't roll it.

"Deal with your own mess," I added after the rock dropped in place. As I walked away from General Treron, I bent down, picked up a candy-bar wrapper from the ground, and tossed it into a trash can. It wasn't much, but it was a start.

TIED UP

It was the bottom of the ninety-seventh inning. We were down by one, 57 to 56. I was up next. Tying run on third, winning run on second. I watched as Kent swung too early at a changeup. Strike three. One out.

"Come on, Tucker," Coach Wagner called from his spot near first base.

I looked at him for some kind of sign. Hit away for the win or sacrifice for the tie? I was pretty sure I could drive Lucas home from third. I might be able to hit a hard grounder and bring Miguel home, too. A win would be good. Wouldn't it?

As I settled down into my batting stance at the plate, I glanced at the scoreboard beyond the left-field fence. It stretched far into the distance. I could barely make out any innings below the thirties. The unplayed innings stretched off to the right.

"Strike!"

Dang. I had to focus. I couldn't let my mind wander.

37

I watched the next pitch come in high and outside. The one after that was also high.

Come on, give me one I can taste. I knew he wouldn't walk me. That would load the bases. Which also meant he wasn't going to risk letting the count get to three and one. Sure enough, he fired a rocket at the upper inside corner of the zone. I halfway decided to swing for the fence, but caution won and I ended up hitting a hopper past first. I was thrown out, but the run scored.

I looked at Coach Wagner. He nodded, but I couldn't tell whether he was really pleased.

"Good job," Kent said when I got back to the bench.

"Thanks." I watched Ethan walk up to the plate. "Maybe I should have gone for the win. What do you think?"

Kent shrugged.

"Hot dogs! Get yer red hots!"

I looked past the fence. A guy was walking by with a small pushcart. I loved hot dogs.

"Here!" I called.

He swung over. I had a couple bucks folded in my sneaker just for this. I traded them for a hot dog.

At the plate, Ethan hit a pop-up. It barely cleared the infield. The shortstop caught it, and the other team came in off the field to start the next inning.

"Come on," Kent said.

"I'll be right there." I gulped the hot dog in three bites. I hated to rush, but I couldn't take it to the field with me. The last bite almost caught in my throat, but I managed to get it down without choking.

"You are such a pig," Kent said. He flashed me a grin. I didn't mind if he kidded me.

"You should talk." I pointed to a ketchup splotch on his pants leg.

He looked down and frowned, then headed over to right field. I noticed he had a couple ketchup stains on his back, too. I jogged out to third base. Top of the ninety-eighth. I'd had at least a couple shots at breaking the tie. But I'd played it safe every time. I guess we all had.

They didn't score any runs that inning. Neither did we. They scored twice in the ninety-ninth inning, but we managed to tie it up again.

"This seems kind of special," I told Kent as we headed into the field for the top of the one hundredth.

"Huh?"

"One hundred innings," I said.

He shrugged. "So?"

"I don't know." I looked around the field. Something was tickling the back of my mind. But this was no time to let my attention wander. I focused on the game. They managed to get one man on but weren't able to advance him. Thanks to a nice dive and throw, I made the third out.

When I came up to bat, I got to first on a walk. I looked at the coach to see if he wanted me to steal.

"Up to you," he said.

I stayed put. After two outs, I made it to third on a strong grounder. If I'd stolen second earlier, the game would be over now. The next batter struck out.

Inning 101. I'd been sure something special would happen at 100.

When we came in for our ups, I asked Kent, "This game seem strange to you?"

He shook his head. "Nope."

"What's the longest you've ever gone with extra innings?"

He frowned. "I don't know. This time, I guess."

"I mean not counting this one." I thought back. Games went ten or eleven innings. Maybe twelve. I wasn't sure what the pro record was, but I was pretty sure it was a lot less than one hundred innings.

"What's the difference?" Kent asked. "I could play all day and be happy."

"Hot dogs!"

The guy with the cart was heading toward us. *Hot dogs*. I always ate them too fast. Choked them down. That's what my mom would say. Mom? I looked around again. The stands were empty. That was weird. My folks always came to my games.

"There's nobody in the stands," I said.

Kent shrugged again. I looked at his back. The red splotches had flowed from dark holes. Bullet wounds.

I gasped. I guess I'd been holding my breath as I stared at Kent's back. I forced myself to search behind the wall that protected me from my memories. I'd grabbed a hot dog before the game. Not this game. Another game. I was up in my room, getting my uniform on. I bit off a hunk and gulped it down as I bent over to lace my cleats.

And realized I couldn't breathe. For an instant, I didn't understand what was wrong. Then panic flooded my body. My parents were downstairs, but I couldn't even make a sound. I tried to get out of the room. That's the last thing I remember.

I knew there was no use talking to Kent. He wasn't ready to remember. Whatever had happened to him, I think it was a lot worse than what happened to me.

But there was someone I could ask. I was leadoff batter in the 103rd inning. They hadn't scored. I got on first, which was just where I wanted to be. I didn't waste words. I might not be on base for long if Ethan got a hit.

I looked over at Coach Wagner. "Am I dead?"

He shook his head. "I don't think so. Not yet."

"So how do I get out of here?" I watched Ethan head for the batter's box.

Coach Wagner sighed. "I was hoping you could tell me." I noticed that his neck was bent at a strange angle. Instead of a regular belt, he was wearing a seat belt.

"We have to win or lose sooner or later. Right?"

"I hope so."

I realized he didn't know any more than I did. But I had to do something.

Or did I? I loved playing ball. I could play forever. I

checked my sock. I had a couple bucks there. I'd always have money for hot dogs. Endless summer.

I glanced back at Coach Wagner. "I'm going to steal."

"It's your call."

"Can you help me?" He might not know all the answers, but he was a coach.

"Yeah. Take a lead."

I moved away from the base and looked back at him.

"One more step," he said. "Then wait for my signal."

He let the first two pitches go. He gave me the signal on the third. I shot toward second and beat the throw.

Ethan dribbled a hit, and I made it to third. Marcus struck out. So did Seth. One more out, and my steal would become meaningless. We'd go into inning 104. And then 105, and eventually 1,000 and 10,000 and on and on.

No way. I loved baseball, but I needed more than that in my life. I watched the first pitch. A ball. As soon as the pitcher went into his windup for the next pitch, I tucked my head and ran like mad. I was going to steal home.

As I got within sliding distance of home plate, I heard the ball smack into the catcher's mitt. I dove for the plate, hoping I could avoid the tag.

An object, hard and round, slammed into my stomach with shocking force.

I tried to slide, but something was holding me up. No, not something. Someone.

My feet dangled. I felt a bunched fist plunge into my

gut again. The hot dog shot from my throat. I gulped air, feeling the dark mist swirl away as my brain drank oxygen.

Dad turned me around and stared at me. "Are you okay?"

I tried to answer, but my throat hurt. I nodded.

His face was pale. "I was so scared," he said. "I thought I'd lost you." Behind him, Mom stood speechless in the hallway.

"I'm here," I whispered.

"Maybe we should skip the game," he said.

I shook my head. "No. I want to play." I'd be all right.

"You sure?"

"Yeah."

As I sat on my bed and caught my breath, I thought about the game I'd left. I figured there'd be a sub for me. There were probably plenty of players. I wondered whether we'd won or lost. Or whether the score was still tied. But I was pretty sure it didn't matter. I didn't get home because I broke the tie. I didn't come back because we'd won or lost. I got home because I wanted it badly enough to do whatever I had to do to get here.

As I walked downstairs, I saw a news bulletin on television. There was a reporter standing in front of a hospital halfway across the country.

"Doctors say he just regained consciousness," the reporter said. There was a small picture in the corner of the screen, with a caption under it. *Innocent bystander shot during holdup.*

43

"Glad you made it, Kent," I whispered. I wondered how many more innings he'd had to go through.

"Ready to play a little ball?" Dad asked.

"Ready to play a lot," I said.

PREDATORS

Mom only lets me go online for an hour each day. "There are a lot of predators out there," she's always saying. I know. The world is full of dangers. But I really need to meet some new people. And the Internet is so much better and faster than anything else.

I hang out at Dark DimenXion. That's a place for fantasy and horror fans. My name is Kirby12. But that's not my real name. I'm too smart to let personal information slip. My real name is Danny. Though the "12" part is sort of accurate.

I made good use of my hour yesterday. I have a new friend. His name is DarkFan43. He told me he's twelve, too. His mom doesn't let him go online very much, either. When I logged on just now, I was afraid he wouldn't be there. But he was. So we chatted. We have a lot in common. He likes all the same stuff I do.

I found out he lives in Milford. That's the next town

over from me. I didn't tell him the name of my town. I'm too smart for that. But I told him I lived near his town.

> DarkFan43: I wish I could spend more time online.
>
> Kirby12: Me, too. It would be fun.
>
> DarkFan43: Too bad we can't hang out.
>
> Kirby12: Yeah.
>
> DarkFan43: Maybe we could meet somewhere.
>
> Kirby12: That would be cool.
>
> DarkFan43: How about the old quarry? Do you live near there?
>
> Kirby12: Yeah. Real close.
>
> DarkFan43: Want to meet me there later today?
>
> Kirby12: My mom won't let me go out.
>
> DarkFan43: She just doesn't want you to have any fun.
>
> Kirby12: That's for sure.
>
> DarkFan43: Could you sneak out at night?
>
> Kirby12: I might get in trouble.
>
> DarkFan43: Come on. Don't be such a baby.
>
> Kirby12: Okay. I'll try.

We decided to meet at the north entrance to the quarry, where the fence is broken, at 10:00. Mom would be busy then. I'd have no trouble sneaking out. The quarry is close enough for me to walk there. I couldn't wait to meet DarkFan.

I arrived early—around 9:45—but someone was already there, standing in the shadows away from the lights by the gate. I walked toward him but stopped when I was still within the pool of light. I wanted to make sure he could see me clearly.

"DarkFan?" I asked.

He nodded. "Kirby?"

"Yup."

"I'm not twelve," he said. "That was a teeny lie."

I'd figured he wasn't a kid the first time we'd talked. Something about him didn't seem right. "I'm twelve," I said. Then I smiled and added, "Centuries."

He gave me a puzzled look. I could tell he wasn't worried. His heart was beating a bit fast, but it wasn't racing, yet.

"Thanks for coming." I tilted my head in the light so he could see my fangs glisten. I love that part. Now his heart was racing. I tried to decide whether to end it quickly or chase him around the quarry for a while. Well, he did say he liked horror. So I guess I knew what his last ten minutes would be like.

He screamed and dashed for the street. I flew past him in a blur, then stopped so he ran into me. He screamed, fell, got up, then scrambled the other way.

I realize Mom doesn't think much of the Internet. But I like it. I can't imagine a better way to meet the right people. It's making the world a smaller place. And a nicer one.

THE CURSE OF THE
CAMPFIRE WEENIES

There are three things I hate to hear from an adult. First, "This will be so much fun." When you hear that, you know it won't. Second, "This is for your own good." No, it isn't. Finally, and worst of all, "Mr. Dwerkin is coming with us."

That third sentence hit me as I was climbing into the back of our van, along with my little brother, Rupert.

"What?" I looked at Dad, hoping I'd heard him wrong.

"I just found out he loves camping, so I invited him along," Dad said. "Don't act so grumpy, Sarah. We have lots of room."

I looked at Mom. She smiled and said, "The poor man is so lonely."

Yeah. For good reason.

Mr. Dwerkin lived next door to us. He was an expert. On everything. You name it, he knew the best and only way to do it. Sometimes I walked all the way around the block just to make sure I didn't run into him. I watched out the window as he dragged piles of camping gear from his garage. He had an awful lot of stuff for one person.

"This stinks," Rupert muttered.

For real. I nodded my head and pinched my nose. That was another thing about Mr. Dwerkin. He smelled like lunch meat. "At least there's a lot of woods to hide in," I whispered to Rupert.

"Hi, kids," Mr. Dwerkin said as he climbed into the van. "I love camping. This is going to be so much fun."

Before we even pulled out of the driveway, he started a sing-along. Did I mention it was a four-hour ride to the campgrounds?

By the time we got there, I couldn't wait to leap out of the van. I shot through the door the instant the opening was wide enough for me to fit. Rupert and I started setting up our tent.

"You're doing it all wrong," Mr. Dwerkin said.

"I like doing things wrong," I said. "It makes me feel special."

"Now, Sarah," Mom said. "Let Mr. Dwerkin show you how to put up your tent."

I sighed and stepped back. Mr. Dwerkin set up the tent all wrong, but I figured I could fix it later.

After we got everything set up, Mom and Dad headed out for a hike. I thought about joining them, but I'm not really big on tromping through the woods. The moment they left, Mr. Dwerkin opened our cooler and dumped all the food onto a blanket. Then he tied up the blanket, tossed one end of the rope over a tree limb, and hoisted everything in the air.

"What are you doing?" I asked.

"Standard woodcraft," he said. "It's important to protect your food from bears. They can catch the scent of a meal from miles away. This way, it's out of their reach."

"Whatever." I grabbed a book from the tent and headed out to sit under a tree and read. Rupert grabbed a coloring book and followed me.

"What are you doing?" Mr. Dwerkin asked.

"Reading."

"No, no, no," Mr. Dwerkin said. "We can't rest yet. We need to gather wood for the campfire."

"There's lots of time for that," I said. "And we don't really need a fire. It's gotta be ninety degrees out here."

He shook his head. "The campfire is the most important part of camping. It's far more than just a source of heat or light. It's the heart of civilization. All other activities revolve around the fire. Everyone knows that." He clapped his hands together. "Come on, don't be lazy campers. Let's go gather wood."

And so Rupert and I gathered wood. Mr. Dwerkin went with us, but he didn't do much gathering. Instead, he examined every single piece we picked up and tossed half of them away. Then he spent at least two hours arranging the wood. At least I got to read while he was doing that. My parents finally returned from their hike, but all they wanted to do was sit around and talk about the plants they'd seen and the birds they'd heard. I wonder if their list included the cuckoo that was jabbering by the woodpile?

When it began to grow dark, Mr. Dwerkin said, "Okay, let's get the campfire lit."

He insisted on starting the fire the old-fashioned way—using a flint and steel. That took another twenty minutes. By then, it was really dark and I was starving.

"All right," Dad said. "Let's bring out those burgers." He bent down and opened the cooler. I could almost see a big question mark floating over his head as he looked into the empty container.

"Where's the food?" he asked.

"Safe from bears," Mr. Dwerkin said, pointing to the bundle dangling from a tree.

"The meat's up there?" Mom asked. "In this heat?"

Mr. Dwerkin nodded.

"How long?" Dad asked.

"All day," Mr. Dwerkin said. "I made it my priority to secure the provisions.

Mom and Dad exchanged glances. I shot them an *I told you so* look, but they ignored me. Then Dad got his car keys. "I hope the market is still open." He and Mom headed for the van.

"We'll go!" Rupert and I screamed. "Take us with you."

"No, it's too long a trip," Dad said. "I don't want you to miss out on the fun. That fire looks fabulous. You kids stay with Mr. Dwerkin."

Mom and Dad scurried off to the van. I watched their

taillights disappear down the road. It was at least forty-five minutes to the closest market. I knew they'd spend far too long shopping. We were stuck with Mr. Dwerkin for at least two hours. Maybe a lot more.

"Let's gather by the fire, kids," Mr. Dwerkin said. "Ancient man huddled by the campfire for safety. All predators fear fire. We'll be safe here." He was carrying a guitar. Before we could even get seated, he started singing "Kumbaya."

"I think we need more wood," I said, leaping to my feet.

"I'll help," Rupert said.

We raced for the woods.

"Kids—it's dangerous to run around in the dark," Mr. Dwerkin called after us.

"We won't go far," I yelled as we fled.

"Hurry back," he said. "I want to tell stories."

We sprinted down a path; then I stopped to catch my breath. "Sheesh, what a weenie," I said.

"Yeah. A total campfire weenie. This is going to be an awful trip," Rupert said.

We weren't really in the dark. I could see other campfires flickering all over the place. Distant sounds of laughter and singing rippled through the woods. The aroma of food drifted our way, making my stomach growl. "Come on, let's find some place to hang out for a while."

We wandered into a clearing. A group of campers—it looked like two sets of parents, with about eight children between them—was cooking something over a fire.

"Come join us, kids," one of the moms called. "We're making yummy gummy gooey hobo stewy." She pointed to a rusty bucket sitting on the fire. Thick bubbles burst on the surface of the brown liquid inside of it.

"And I'm making cherry berry piekins," a little girl said, grinning a gap-toothed smile and holding up a can of biscuits and a jar of jam. She sneezed, then wiped her nose with her arm.

"Uh, no thanks." Rupert and I backed away.

The next spot we found seemed a lot safer. It was a troop of Girl Scouts. The leader invited us to join them at the fire.

"This looks better," Rupert said.

"It'll be fine," I said.

But then they started singing.

"Yibby dibby boopsie doopsie. Walla wango bimmy gap!"

"Huh?" Rupert whispered.

"Campfire song," I explained.

"Zoomy gloomy, walla woomie, give your head a snap!"

With each line, they made strange gestures with their hands. Rupert looked at me. I shrugged. I'd been a Girl Scout for three weeks, once. I forgot they were so big on weird songs and hand gestures.

The second verse was the same as the first. So was the third. And the twentieth. By then, I was ready to rip my yibby dibby ears off my walla wango head.

I snuck away from the firelight, pulling Rupert with me. None of the girls seemed to notice. As we escaped, we could hear them singing a new song in the distance. This one was a list of fast-food restaurants, beginning with Pizza Hut. I could just imagine the hand gestures.

"Mr. Dwerkin isn't looking all that bad," Rupert said.

"Yeah. At least he hasn't sneezed on our food yet. Let's head back. We'll survive, as long as we sit upwind of him." A day in the woods hadn't helped the whole lunch-meat thing.

I followed the sound of his guitar back to our campsite.

"Awesome. You got here just in time. The fire's perfect. We're ready for my favorite part. Let's tell scary stories."

"No!" Rupert clamped his hands on his ears. "I don't like scary stories."

"Maybe tomorrow." I stood up again and looked at the tent. Going to sleep early and hungry would be better than listening to some ridiculous story.

"You can't go to sleep and waste this great fire," Mr. Dwerkin said. "Besides—while your parents are away, I'm in charge." He walked over and pulled Rupert's hands away from his ears. "And I say we're telling scary stories."

I thought about running away. But there was nothing around us except all sorts of campfire weenies cooking weird stuff, singing mind-numbing songs, and melting marshmallows into submission.

"It will be okay," I whispered to Rupert as Mr. Dwerkin took a seat. "He'll just tell us one of those old stupid urban myth things and then scream at the end."

"This really happened," Mr. Dwerkin said. He leaned close to the fire, so the flames made him look even creepier than normal. "This boy took this girl out on a date. And they went off to park on the side of the road. Then the boy turned on the radio, and they heard that an escaped killer was out there. But guess what?"

"He had a hook for a hand?" I guessed.

Mr. Dwerkin glared at me. "Hey, who's telling the story? Me or you?"

"Sorry," I said.

"Can you listen for five minutes without interrupting?" Mr. Dwerkin asked.

"Sure."

"Promise?"

I nodded. Mr. Dwerkin looked at Rupert. He nodded, too.

Mr. Dwerkin started telling a new story. "There's an empty house next to a graveyard at the end of a dead-end street."

That's when I noticed the trees rustling behind him. A dark shape moved into view.

"A bear!" I screamed.

"Nice try," Mr. Dwerkin said. "But leave the spooky stories to the experts. And please stop interrupting."

"But—"

"I said stop interrupting." He stared at me for a moment, then continued with the story. "My friends dared me to go into the house. . . ."

I got up. So did Rupert. I backed away a step. So did Rupert. "There's really a bear behind you," I said, pointing to the shape that was rising up a foot or two away from Mr. Dwerkin and batting at the dangling sack of food.

Rupert pointed, too. "Honest. Just look."

"Right. I'm going to fall for that old trick from a couple kids who don't even know how to build a campfire. No way. Besides, bears are afraid of fire. Now, will you let me finish?"

I backed off a couple more steps. The bear gave up on the sack. It went back on all fours and sniffed the air, then looked over at Mr. Dwerkin and licked its snout. It didn't seem to be scared of the fire at all.

"I'm not going to let you miss the story," Mr. Dwerkin said. "You need to finish what you start. And show some respect for your elders. It's for your own good." He started shouting the story. I guess he was determined to make sure we heard it.

Rupert and I scurried farther into the woods, but we were still close enough to hear the ending.

"And then I saw the ghost!" Mr. Dwerking shouted. "And the ghost grabbed me and then . . ."

"Is this where he screams?" Rupert asked.

"Probably."

"I became the ghost!" Mr. Dwerkin shouted. The end of the story was followed by a scream. It was a loud scream and a long one. A lot longer than I'd expected.

"Stupid story," I said. "But I have to admit, the scream was pretty good."

"Yeah. That's the one part of it he did right. But I'm still not going back right now."

"Me, either. Want to go see what the Girl Scouts are doing?"

"You think they're done singing?" Rupert asked.

"Nah. Those songs last forever. But at least they don't act like they know everything."

"Yeah. And they don't smell like lunch meat."

CAT NAPPED

LET ME GO, YOU WRETCHED BEAST!"

The shout came from the backyard.

Oswald heard it through the open window in his bedroom. As he ran down the steps and out the back door, he wondered about the voice. It was loud but small.

Oswald had no trouble finding the source. The shouting kept on, nonstop, from under the dogwood tree. Raffi, Oswald's gray tabby cat, stood there with her prey dangling from her jaws.

The prey was the source of the loud-but-small shouts. The prey himself was loud but small.

"Wow," Oswald said. The tiny guy in the green suit had to be a leprechaun. No mistake.

Raffi had the collar of the leprechaun's green coat clamped in her jaws.

"WRETCHED BEAST!" the captive shouted.

Oswald, who was no fool in these things, leaped straight

to the point. "I get a pot of gold, right? Isn't that the deal? I let you go, and you give me gold."

The leprechaun glared at him.

"Come on, is that it?" Oswald asked.

Raffi shook her head, rattling the leprechaun around like an empty glove.

"STOP THAT!" the leprechaun shouted. "All right, I'll give you gold, but you have to provide the pot."

"What?" Oswald didn't understand.

"The pot, you dim-witted foul-breathed monster," the leprechaun said. "Go get a pot, I'll fill it with gold, and we'll be done with the whole thing."

"Deal." Oswald ran into the kitchen and searched through the cabinets. There were tons of pots, pans, skillets, and bowls. But they weren't big enough. Oswald knew the pot he wanted—the pot his mom used when she made soup. He imagined how it would look filled with gold. That would be an awful lot of treasure.

He spotted the pot. It was sitting on the kitchen counter, filled with vegetables and a big soup bone. *Mom must be making soup*, he thought. With all the gold he was about to get, he could buy his mom a truckload of soup. Luckily, she hadn't turned on the burner yet, so the pot was cold. Oswald dumped the vegetables in the sink and went running out the back door, eager to get the pot filled with gold.

Raffi was still under the tree. But there was no sign of the leprechaun.

"Huh?" Oswald stared at Raffi for a moment. Then he noticed something on the ground next to his cat. "Oh no." Oswald recognized the label. He dropped the pot, bent over, and grabbed the can.

"You made a deal with him, didn't you?" Oswald said, waving the can of tuna in front at Raffi. "You let him go for this. One stupid little can of tuna. And you can't even open it. Unbelievable. You are such a stupid animal." Oswald threw the can to the ground and stomped back into the kitchen—just in time to run into his mother, who was very interested in hearing his explanation for the sink full of vegetables.

Outside, Raffi waited beneath the dogwood tree. In a moment, the leprechaun came walking out from under the bushes, dragging a can opener.

"Here you go," he said as he tossed the opener in front of the cat. "A deal's a deal. Don't pay any attention to that silly human. You aren't stupid. Not at all. You're a very smart kitty cat." With that, the leprechaun chuckled and skittered away.

Raffi batted at the opener with her left front paw. It didn't do any good. Then she batted it for a while with her right front paw. It still didn't do any good. Eventually, Raffi gave up and went off in search of mice. They tasted better than tuna, anyhow.

THE UNFORGIVING TREE

It was on a Thursday just two weeks after school ended that Ricky noticed the tree had moved. It hadn't moved a lot and there were no obvious signs that anything had happened, but Ricky knew right away that the tree wasn't where it had always been.

It was easy for him to tell. He liked to stand with his back against the tree and bounce a ball against the house. He'd been doing it for so many years that he knew right away when something was wrong. Either the tree had moved or the house had moved.

Ricky was pretty sure the house hadn't moved.

He started checking the tree each day. He measured the distance from the tree to the house. The tape didn't seem to show any change from one day to the next, but Ricky could tell that the tree was getting closer. He didn't mention anything to his parents. They wouldn't believe him. He was sure of that.

But he kept an eye on the tree. By the middle of the summer, he was positive that it had gotten a lot closer to the house. That wouldn't have been so bad, but the tree was right outside his bedroom window.

It wanted something. He was sure of that.

One night, a branch got so close that it broke his window. His parents came running.

"Why'd you do it?" his father asked.

"I didn't," Ricky said. He looked down and saw proof of his innocence. There was glass on the floor. "See," he said, pointing to the shards. "It was broken from the outside. Otherwise, the glass would be on the ground."

"Don't try to act innocent," his father said. "That window is coming out of your allowance." He stomped downstairs, then came back with a piece of cardboard that he taped over the broken pane.

Ricky went back to bed and lay there listening to the sound of branches tapping against the side of the house. He looked out through the unbroken part of the window. There was no breeze that night.

The next morning, Ricky measured the distance from the house. The tree was three feet away. Ricky hadn't checked for a week or so, but he was sure that the last time he'd measured the tree, it had been four feet away.

"Dad, that tree is moving closer to the house," Ricky said during breakfast.

"Of course it is," his father said, glancing up from the newspaper. "It's growing. I remember when we moved here—that tree was just a scrawny sapling. Now look at it. I'd bet it's at least thirty feet high. I still can't believe it survived that little stunt you pulled with the saw."

"What stunt?" Ricky asked.

His father grinned. "Don't you remember?"

"Nope."

"Well, you were pretty young. But you'd gotten your hands on one of my saws, and you were doing a good job of cutting the tree down. I managed to catch you just in time. A couple more minutes and you would have cut so deep that the tree would never have recovered. I'm surprised you don't remember. You got quite a spanking that day."

Ricky thought back. He had vague memories of being punished for something when he was little, but all of that was a long time ago. It didn't matter. His real problem was in the present.

"The tree's not just growing," he said. "It's getting closer to the house."

His father mumbled, "That's nice," and kept reading the paper.

Ricky went outside to look at the tree again. A foot and a half above the ground, he saw a long scar in the trunk.

"Hey, I'm sorry. That was years ago. I was just a kid. Can't you forget about it?"

Ricky stood there for a moment, almost expecting to get some kind of answer. Then he realized how foolish he sounded talking to a tree. But there was one more thing he had to tell it. "You won't get me," Ricky said, "I can move faster than you."

He stepped away, then jumped as a branch crashed to the ground on the spot where he'd been standing.

That night, Ricky heard his window sliding open. A branch poked through the gap. He grabbed his pocketknife from his desk and hacked at the branch. Something brown gushed from the cut and spilled over his hands. The branch pulled back outside.

Ricky slammed the window shut, then went to wash his hands. When he came back into his room, the window was open again. Ricky decided to go sleep on the couch in the living room. But he stopped by the door. "No. This is my room. Nothing is going to scare me out of it." He turned back toward the tree. "You aren't going to win."

Ricky sat on his bed and watched the branch. It was still growing, moving deeper into his room. But it was moving slowly. At some point Ricky fell asleep. He woke late the next morning. His window was open, but there was no sign of the branch. In the middle of his room, halfway from the window to his bed, Ricky saw a leaf lying on the floor.

Why now? Ricky wondered. The incident with the saw had happened so long ago. He'd once heard his father say that a wise man waits three years for vengeance. Were trees more patient than that?

Ricky closed the window. As he looked at the tree, he knew he had to do something. He had to do it before bedtime. When night came, the tree would get even closer, maybe too close.

After checking to make sure his parents weren't around,

Ricky went to the garage and searched through his dad's tools. The saws were all too small for the job. There was an ax, but it was too heavy. Ricky looked for something else he could use. He thought about the shovel, but there was no way he could dig deep enough to remove the tree.

As he stood there, trying to think of something he could use, he heard his parents pulling into the driveway. It was too late. He'd have to find something else. For now, there were no answers in the garage.

Ricky went back outside. The tree was even closer to the house now. He was sure of that. He had to get rid of it.

Ricky sat in the yard, watching the tree, half-expecting to see it move. He was startled to hear his mother shouting for his father. "Fred! There's water in the basement!"

Ricky followed his father downstairs. Sure enough, there was a large puddle on the floor of the basement and wet spots on the wall.

"Tree roots," Ricky's father said after examining the problem. "They're growing through the foundation."

"I told you it was getting close to the house," Ricky said.

His father ignored him. But the next thing his father said thrilled Ricky. "Nothing to do but get the tree cut down."

Ricky let out a cheer, not caring at all about the strange look he got in return. That night, he stayed awake and huddled in a corner of his room as a probing branch made it almost all the way to his bed. But the next day he had the pleasure of watching while a crew of men came and cut down the tree.

It was over.

"Yup," his father said, walking over next to Ricky, "I'll never forget that day you got your hands on my saw. Or the time you used your pocketknife to carve your initials on every tree around here."

"Every tree?" It had been so long ago. But it came back to him. Ricky remembered when he had done that. He'd been six, so it must have been about a year after the incident with the saw. He looked around the yard. There were so many trees. And they all seemed closer to the house than before—a lot closer than he remembered.

"Yup," Ricky's father said. "Every tree. It's amazing what you kids think you can get away with."

All around him. Ricky heard the rustle of branches moving in the wind and the creak of roots straining against the soil.

BOBBING FOR DUMMIES

This is so pathetic," Arnold said as he looked around the room. He couldn't believe he'd given up trick or treat for a stupid Halloween party at the YMCA. Especially a party crawling with little kids.

But his mom hadn't offered him a choice. She believed Halloween was a dangerous holiday and that kids shouldn't be "roaming from house to house, pleading for candy like a bunch of beggars." So it was the party or nothing.

At least his friend Lewis was there. Lewis really knew how to have fun. Better yet, the woman who was in charge had just stepped out of the all-purpose room to go get more soda.

"Let's wreck this," Lewis whispered to Arnold.

"Sure." Arnold looked around for something to wreck. But Lewis was way ahead of him. He stuck his head in the bucket where apples bobbed and sucked up a big mouthful of water. Then he spat the water back into the bucket.

"Who wants to bob?" Lewis asked, grinning.

A little boy toddled up to them. "I wanna bob."

"Go away," Arnold said, giving the kid a push. "You're too small to bob."

"No, he's not," Lewis said. He lifted the kid and dumped him in the water. "See, he bobs just fine."

"You're right. But he cries a lot, too." Arnold moved away from the wet, noisy kid. "This is getting boring. Let's do something else."

Arnold looked around the room at the little kids in their stupid costumes. When he spotted a boy who was dressed as a turkey, he grabbed Lewis's arm and said, "Let's make a wish."

"Yeah!"

They raced over and each grabbed a leg, like it was one end of a wishbone.

"I wish this party wasn't so stupid," Lewis said.

Arnold glanced over at the bobbing bucket, where the wet kid was still crying. "I wish bobbing wasn't so boring." He tugged at the boy's leg.

The boy screamed. Lewis dropped his leg. "Guess I win," Arnold said. But he was bored again. These kids were no fun to pick on. They just crumpled up and cried. It was too easy. Arnold dropped the boy's other leg. "Now what?"

"Dessert!" Lewis attacked the snacks, taking one bite out of each brownie. Arnold joined him, licking a bare stripe across the top of each cupcake.

Just as they were finishing their snack, the woman in charge of the party returned and asked them to leave. Actually, she did more than ask. She demanded. Loudly.

Fine with me, Arnold thought as he left the room.

"Hey," Lewis said, "let's go swimming."

"I think the pool's closed," Arnold said.

"Nothing's ever closed," Lewis told him. "That's what I always say. Come on."

They slipped into the pool. It might have been closed, but it wasn't locked.

"That really was a lousy party," Arnold said as he floated on his back in the middle of the pool.

"Really lousy," Lewis agreed. "Stupid games. Bobbing for apples. That's no fun. Bobbing is for babies."

"Totally boring." Arnold stared at the ceiling. As he gazed up there, something tore the roof off, exposing the pool to the night sky.

Giant heads appeared at the edges of the walls. Giant hands gripped the tops of the wall. One head pushed down toward the pool. Arnold screamed as the clamping teeth just missed him.

The head rose, then plunged down again. It got Lewis. Another head bobbed down. Arnold tried to reach the side of the pool. He never made it. But he got his wish. Briefly, very briefly, bobbing was definitely not boring.

EAT A BUG

Laura stood at the edge of the playground, watching the other kids. This wasn't a good day. Sometimes someone would need an extra hand to turn a jump rope or an extra body to balance a seesaw. Not today. There was an empty seesaw, but Laura knew that it wouldn't do any good to go over there. She was sure she could sit all day and all night and all the rest of her life and not a single kid would bother to take the other end.

Laura didn't know why things were this way. *It could be worse*, she told herself, looking across the playground. *At least I'm not Debbie Dirt-Digger.* Laura took some small satisfaction in knowing that there was one person even lonelier than she was. She watched as Debbie knelt in the dirt on the other side of the playground and dug with a stick.

Every day at recess, Debbie walked past the slides and swing and seesaw, continued past the backstop, and went into the far corner of the playground. When she got there, she picked up a stick and dug in the dirt. It was so much a part of the playground routine that Laura rarely thought of it anymore. Even the meanest kids had grown tired of taunting her. As Laura looked at Debbie, she almost felt sorry for her.

Suddenly Debbie raised her head. Her eyes locked with Laura's.

Laura wanted to look away. But that would mean losing some unspoken contest to Debbie. Maybe even moving below Debbie, all the way to the bottom of the invisible social ranking that followed Laura through school. There was no way she'd let that happen. She held the other girl's gaze.

Debbie smiled. The smile reminded Laura of a caterpillar stretching across a half-dried leaf.

Laura found herself walking past the slides and swing and seesaw and around the backstop. She felt as if she were being tugged through air as thick as syrup. She stood above Debbie.

"Hi," Debbie said, still smiling. There didn't appear to be any happiness in her expression.

"Uh, hi," Laura said.

"You don't have any friends," Debbie said.

Stung by the blunt truth, Laura struck back. "Neither do you."

"Yes, I do."

Laura didn't bother to answer. It would be ridiculous to argue about something so obvious.

"I'll be your friend if you eat a bug," Debbie said.

Laura was sure that she'd heard wrong. "What?"

Still looking at Laura, Debbie scratched at the dirt with her stick. "Eat a bug," she said. Then she giggled. "It's no big deal. Birds do it all the time. So do shrews and moles. Eat a bug. Just one. Then I'll be your friend."

This is ridiculous, Laura thought, but she knelt next to Debbie. A *friend* . . . A *bug* . . . Laura couldn't look away from those eyes. At the edges of her vision, she was aware that Debbie had stopped digging and was taking something from the hole.

Debbie's hand came forward. "Friends," she whispered. She cradled something in her fist.

Laura, her eyes locked on Debbie's, reached out. She flinched for an instant as a soft and wriggling thing touched her palm.

"Quickly," Debbie said.

Laura's hand moved toward her mouth. It was over in an instant, so quick she swallowed before she could even shudder.

"Did you chew?" Debbie asked.

Laura shook her head, then said, "No." That would have been too awful. She wiped her hand on her shirt.

Debbie, her eyes still holding Laura, nodded. "Good. If you do that, they can't lay their eggs."

"What?"

"Nothing," Debbie said. "Don't think about it. You'll have friends soon, lots of friends. And so will I. So will everyone. Bugs are so much nicer than people. They treat everyone the same." She looked away.

As Laura lost Debbie's gaze, the world seemed to fade for an instant. When it returned, Laura was standing across the playground, watching the girl dig in the dirt. Laura frowned and brushed a small speck of dirt off her fingertip. For a moment, she thought she had just eaten a bug. But that couldn't be. No, she'd never do something like that. Her stomach fluttered at the very idea. Her stomach fluttered and wriggled.

Across the playground, Debbie hummed as she dug in the dirt.

THROWAWAYS

It's a good thing the garbagemen didn't have one of those trucks that crush everything. Of course, I never figured things would go that far. When Dad tossed me into the can and carried me out to the curb, I thought he'd just let me stay there for a little while. It's not like I'd done anything really bad. All I did was play with his autographed Yankee baseball. I hardly got it a tiny bit smudged.

So I figured he'd be out sooner or later. I couldn't go back in. He'd said, "Stay there," and I didn't want to end up in more trouble by disobeying. Then it got dark.

At least it didn't get too chilly that night.

The garbage truck showed up just before sunrise. The noise woke me. I guess I was sleeping pretty soundly. I'm glad I woke, though. The sky was turning from black to red and purple. It was really pretty.

The garbagemen didn't even look at me twice. They just lifted the can and chucked me in the back of the truck. They've probably seen all sorts of things waiting for them on the curb.

I watched out for Dad as we drove away. I was sort of hoping he'd come after the truck and explain that it was all a mistake.

He didn't.

The dump turned out to be a lot nicer than I'd expected. It hardly smelled at all. Of course, I just might have been used to the smell by the time I got there, since the truck picked up a lot of garbage. There weren't any other kids, but I saw a couple of old televisions and an accordion.

The truck dumped everything at the edge of this huge mountain of garbage. I had to push my way out, but there was nothing heavy on top of me, mostly just food and paper and that kind of stuff, so it wasn't too hard to dig myself free. People sure threw out a lot of food.

I figured this was going to be it for me—I'd have to stay in the dump. But two or three minutes after the garbage truck left, the scavengers came by. They were driving an old, banged-up pickup truck. They stopped right next to me and one of them said, "Hey, look. Somebody threw out a perfectly good kid."

"Well," the other said, "don't just stand there. Grab him."

So I found myself in another truck. They took me to a building and hosed me off. Then they tossed me back in the truck, along with other stuff they'd rescued from the dump, and drove to this big outdoor market.

They put me between a gas grill and a rocking chair. The grill had some rust on it, but it looked like it still worked. The chair was scratched up and the paint was chipped in several places, but the wood seemed solid. I felt pretty good. They could have stuck me with the old dishes and other cheap junk. Being with the grill and the chair helped raise my self-esteem.

A little later, a man and woman came along.

"Oh look, Horace," the woman said, pointing at me.

"We have a rocking chair, Emily," the man said.

"No, not the chair, next to it," the woman said.

"Oh yeah. The boy. Hmmmm." The man walked over and stooped down. He looked at me for a while, then nodded at the woman. He talked to the guy about the price, and they argued a bit, but not too much. Then Horace pulled out his wallet and handed over some money.

Horace and Emily took me home.

I like it here. I pretty much behave myself. Horace doesn't own any autographed Yankee baseballs. But if he did, I'd try really hard not to play with them. I might not be so lucky next time.

TOUCH THE BOTTOM

They say Greenhill Lake doesn't have a bottom. They say the deepest spot, straight below dead center, goes down forever. As long as I can remember, we've been coming to the lake for vacation. We rented a cabin there every summer. It's always pretty much the same. Dad and his buddies sat at a table under a tree and played poker. Mom and the other women talked or read. My friends and I spent the days swimming or hiking through the woods.

The lake wasn't very big. I could swim across it the long way without getting tired. And the middle was easy to find. Joey Devon taught me how to do it. You swam out until you could see the white birch along the south bank. You had to line the birch up with the radio tower on the mountain. That got you in the middle, as far as east and west. Then you had to look west and line up the chimney of the third cabin with the sign on the highway. When all of that was lined up, you were right smack in the middle of the lake.

That morning, I'd paddled out there on my blow-up raft. I was drifting around with my eyes closed when I got flipped. Once a raft is half flipped over, it's all over. There's no way to stop it, no matter how hard you fight.

So I gave up and tumbled into the water.

Joey's laugh greeted me when I came back up. I dunked him. Then we splashed each other until my arms got tired. I guess that wore him out as much as me, because we hung on to my raft and floated for a while, letting the sun bake us into contented lumps of warm laziness. On the shore by the cabin I saw my father chase off a couple geese with a handful of gravel.

"Enough of this lazy stuff," Joey said. "I'm going to do it. Right now. I'm going for the bottom."

"You're crazy," I told him.

"Watch me." Joey took a deep breath, let go of the raft, then jackknifed down. I watched until the murk swallowed his legs from view.

Just for fun, I held my breath, too. I knew I could go longer than Joey. It was easier for me because I didn't have to waste any energy forcing myself through the water. Sure enough, well before I felt the urge to breathe, Joey burst back through the surface, gasping.

"Told you," I said.

"Told me nothing," he said. "Look what I have." He held out his fist, clenched shut. Then, slowly, like a magician performing a coin trick, he unfolded his fingers.

Dark, gritty globs dripped from his palm and plopped into the water.

Mud.

Bottom mud.

"No way," I said, not believing what I saw.

Joey just grinned.

That's when I noticed something floating next to him. "You faker," I said, grabbing the plastic bag. Sure enough, there was a trace of mud left in the bottom. Joey must have tucked it inside his swimsuit before he swam out.

"Got ya, sucker."

I shook my head. "You didn't fool me for a minute."

"Yes, I did. I thought your eyes would pop out when I showed you that mud."

"Maybe you had me for a second or two." I figured I could give him that much. He'd worked hard to pull off the trick. I had to admit it was pretty clever. I wished it weren't a trick. It would be great to touch the bottom for real. Too bad we didn't have some kind of air tank. I looked at the plastic bag. Maybe there was a way. I opened up the bag, then closed it, trapping air inside.

"I'm going to do it," I said.

"What?" Joey asked.

"Make it to the bottom." I took a couple of deep breaths, then swam under the water.

As I suspected, the bag was tough to bring down, but I hadn't filled it too much. I swam as hard as I could, pulling myself deeper and deeper. When I thought my lungs would explode, I exhaled as much as I could; then I put the bag to my lips, pinched my nose, and breathed in the air I'd brought with me.

The bag gave me barely enough for a short gasp. It was a lot less than I'd expected. I sucked out all the air, then let the bag go and stroked hard.

I knew I'd never been this far before. It was totally dark. I pushed deeper, hoping my fingers would meet mud or sand or even rock. I thought about the time last year we'd found a bluegill at the edge of the lake, gasping weakly as it drowned in the air. While the adults had stood around watching, Joey had stepped forward and put the fish back in the water.

My lungs burned. I knew I'd have to turn away at any instant—the farther down I went, the longer it would take me to get back up. I'd reached my limit. Maybe next time, or next year, I'd make it.

That's when I saw the glow.

Dim, weak, barely there. I blinked, wondering whether my air-starved brain was playing tricks on me. I'd read that divers start to see stuff if they go too deep or stay down too long. But tricks don't get this real.

The glow grew stronger, became a light.

The light surrounded a moving form, maybe ten feet below me.

I nearly screamed. That scream would have filled my lungs with water and cost me my life. I clamped my jaw so hard I thought my molars would crack.

The creature had arms and legs. But no hands or feet. The limbs ended in tentacles. It struggled upward, whip-

ping at the water, slowly pulling itself higher, like someone climbing a steep hill. As it got closer, I realized it was
huge—at least three or four times as big as a person. Our
eyes locked. It stared at me with large, round orbs of
white, each speckled with a thousand pupils that dilated
at the sight of me. Intelligent eyes. I couldn't pretend this
was a dumb sea creature—not when its waist was wrapped
in fabric that was fastened with a wide belt. Not when it
wore an intricately braided band of metal around one
tentacle.

The last tiny bubble of air spilled from my mouth.

Below me, a stream of something drifted from a slit beneath the creature's eyes. Mud, silt, some form of earth.

I'd come as far as I could, as deep as possible.

As I turned and stroked for the surface, I saw the creature do the same, heading back to whatever world it
dwelled in beneath the bottom, its dense body dropping
just as my buoyant body rose.

We shared a common failed effort.

I'd failed to reach the bottom.

It had failed to reach the surface.

The pale body reminded me of the time I'd been hiking with my uncle Ron. When we'd stopped to rest, I'd
reached down and lifted a fallen log. Dozens of larvae
wriggled on the exposed ground, blind and helpless. Before I could put the log back, Uncle Ron picked up a rock
and smashed the life out of them.

I broke through to the surface and let the clean, sweet
air above the lake fill my lungs.

"Make it?" Joey asked.

I shook my head, too winded to speak.

"That's what I thought," he said. "We're never going to get to the bottom."

I grabbed onto the edge of the raft and drank deep gulps of air. On the bank near the shore, our parents talked and played their adult games. I watched Dad throw a rock at another goose. Somewhere below us, creatures breathed mud and made their own light. They looked so different from us, but I was afraid we had a lot in common.

"Never reach it," Joey said again.

"Maybe not." But I knew we'd keep trying. And so would they. All I hoped was that the creature who finally reached us would be a kid like me.

THE GENIE OF THE NECKLACE

Karen fought with Stacy over the necklace. She knew she'd seen it first, even though she was halfway across the shop when she spotted it. Stacy had no right to try to grab it before she could get there.

They'd ended up tugging at the necklace, pulling hard, yanking, until Karen was afraid the chain would break. But it held. It was a strong chain, made of hundreds of tiny links. It was a long, beautiful chain, from which hung the most lovely green stone Karen had ever seen.

"It's mine," Karen said. "I want it. I saw it first. You know I love silver."

"Oh, all right." Stacy released her end. She turned away from Karen and picked up a tie-dyed scarf from another table. "This is a lot nicer, anyhow."

Karen ran her fingers over the chain, then stroked the polished surface of the wonderful green stone that hung from it. The gem was the size of a robin's egg. She was sure the color perfectly matched her eyes. Karen smiled as she realized she'd won the battle. She usually won her battles with Stacy.

But could she afford it?

She checked the price tag. *This can't be right,* Karen thought as her delight wrestled with suspicion. She approached the owner of the shop, who sat behind the counter working on a crossword puzzle.

"Excuse me," Karen said, her voice sounding strangely empty in this dusty place of ancient objects.

"Yes?"

"This is twelve dollars, right?"

The man nodded.

Karen couldn't believe her luck. Quickly, before anything could change, she paid for the necklace.

"Would you like a bag?" the man asked as he placed her change on the counter.

"I'll wear it," she said, fastening the necklace around her neck.

As she put it on, she glanced into a grimy, cracked mirror on an old dresser. She couldn't help smiling. The necklace looked beautiful. And so did she.

"You have to admit, I was born to wear this," she told Stacy as they left the shop.

"Yeah," Stacy mumbled as she tied the scarf on her head.

"Hey, you still angry?" Karen asked.

Stacy shook her head. "Not really."

"Good." Karen couldn't wait to get to her room so she could admire the necklace in a clean mirror.

She said good-bye to Stacy and hurried home.

Later, Karen was pretty sure it had been a combination of things that had released the creature. The mirror might have played a part. And perhaps the perfume she'd dribbled on her neck. Stroking the gem must have done something—like stroking Aladdin's lamp. Maybe the tune she'd been humming even played a role.

Whatever the cause, the result happened quickly. One instant, Karen was alone in her room, admiring her purchase. The next, a jet of green steam shot from the gem and splashed against the mirror. A thick and clotted liquid formed on the glass, oozing down onto her dresser, covering most of the surface and then rising, taking shape, growing into a creature perhaps two feet high and almost as wide.

Karen was too shocked to scream. She stood, silently trembling, watching as the creature took final form, solidifying, becoming almost more real than she could bear. He had a large head, as wide as his shoulders, and massive hands that drooped all the way down to his feet. He opened his mouth and hissed. He reached out with one hand, tipped with jagged nails, and started to swipe at her as if he wanted to rip her face off.

Then he stopped.

Karen could tell he was staring at the gem.

And that was when she knew she was at a crossroad. The necklace, and this creature, could be either the greatest thing that ever happened to her or the worst. This was deep, secret magic that could help her or hurt her. If she was smart and brave, the world could be hers. If she was foolish, she was sure she would suffer.

"The gem," she said. "You can't hurt me when I wear the gem. Is that right?"

"Yes," the creature said in a voice that sounded like acid eating through metal.

"You must obey my orders. Right?" She was sure of it.

"Yes."

"What can you do for me?" Karen asked.

"Anything you desire, I can get. Anywhere you wish to be, I can take you," the creature said. "I can do anything except change the past or break a bargain."

"Then I would like—" Karen stopped. There had to be a catch. There had to be a cost. She'd read too many fairy tales to believe otherwise. "What must I give in return?" she asked, proud of her cleverness. She knew most people would never have thought to ask this crucial question.

The creature reached to his side and touched a small gold candlestick that stood on the edge of the dresser. He scraped his nail along the base, shaving off a gleaming sliver.

"Hey, you're scratching it," Karen said.

The creature ignored her protest and held his hand out. "A small payment," he said. "A tiny piece of gold." He stared down at his hand, as if weighing the metal. "Just this much. Each day."

Karen looked at the candlestick. The shaving was very small. It was nothing. What harm could there be? Karen smiled as she realized how stupid this creature was. He could scratch that candlestick as much as he wanted. It wouldn't matter. All she had to do was ask for another one. But she was also proud of her ability to strike a bargain. There was no way she'd let him have what he wanted.

"Not gold," she said. She pointed to another candlestick. "Silver."

The creature glared at her without speaking. Karen realized she was in control. The feeling of power made her shiver. *I've won*, she thought. She waited, knowing the creature would accept.

Still glaring, he said, "Very well. A tiny piece of silver. Do we have a bargain?"

Karen nodded, then said, "Bring me a perfect strawberry."

It was winter. There was no good fresh fruit at the local market.

The creature nodded. "As you wish."

He melted into the floor. An instant later, he returned, holding one perfect red strawberry in his claws.

Karen took the berry carefully, avoiding any contact with the creature's skin. As she placed the fruit in her mouth, she felt as if the act of eating the strawberry was sealing her forever in a bargain with this creature. She quickly forgot such thoughts as she bit into the fruit. It tasted wonderful.

"What shall I call you?" she asked.

"Izma," the creature replied.

"Fetch me another strawberry, Izma," Karen said.

Fruit by fruit, she ate her fill, then grew tired of the game. She gazed out the window at the cold land. "Take me somewhere lovely and warm."

Izma performed a series of motions with his claws. The world flew past Karen and she found herself on a beach. She stood for a moment, blinking against the brightness and enjoying the wonderful warmth of the tropical sun and the soft crunch of pure white sand beneath her feet.

"Bathing suit," she said, and Izma caused her to be dressed in clothing more suited to the beach.

"Chair." Karen stretched, drank in the sun, and thought about all the marvelous things she could do from this day forward. And she thought how her friends would be rewarded and how her enemies would finally suffer.

Life was certainly on its way to becoming fabulous.

"What can you do to my enemies?" Karen asked.

Izma told her.

Karen shuddered. Then she smiled.

That evening, tanned from the sun and filled with the peace of the ocean, Karen slept well.

The next day, she began reshaping the world. She sent her parents away. They weren't needed anymore. She took her name off the school roster. But that didn't seem like a good enough way to leave her old world behind. So she went to school, stood outside the teachers' lounge, and commanded, "Turn the teachers into frogs."

The frogs weren't very interesting or exciting. "Turn the boys into snakes," Karen said.

That seemed to get the attention of the frogs and of the girls.

After Karen returned to the beach, she decided that none of her friends really deserved anything. What had they ever done for her?

She got a mansion, a castle, a palace, and a penthouse suite. She got a hundred cats. Then she tired of them and got a dozen tigers.

But always, each day, as she made her wishes, she could see one thing in Izma's eyes. He was waiting for her to make a mistake. He was waiting for her to remove the gem that protected her. One slip, and the dream would become a nightmare. She'd seen Izma chase down small animals and do horrible things to them.

Karen knew she was too smart to become his victim.

A month passed, and Karen was sure that, unlike others who might grow bored with luxury and a perfect life, she would be happy forever. There was so much to do, so much to try. So many people who deserved to suffer. The world was hers.

She stood in the bedroom of her palace, admiring herself in the mirror. Maybe she would go to see the pyramids today or perhaps the rain forest. Then one flaw caught her eye, and all thoughts of travel fell from her mind like dead leaves.

At first, she didn't understand. Or didn't want to understand. She stared at a small patch of untanned skin just below her neck. The spot was the same shape as her gem. But it wasn't where it should have been.

The patch was lower than the gem. Which meant the gem had moved higher. There was only one way that could happen.

Karen's right hand flew to her neck, clutching the gem, almost ripping it off.

She froze as she heard a hiss of anticipation from the corner of the room, where Izma stood awaiting her wishes.

"No," Karen said aloud. *This isn't happening. It's just my imagination.*

But that night, as she lay in bed, she counted the tiny links. She counted them again the next night. She counted twice to make sure.

And she counted them again the night after that.

There was no mistake. A link had vanished from her chain each day.

A tiny piece of silver.

The words came back to her. He'd asked for gold, but she'd cleverly forced him to accept less than he'd wanted. Karen sat up in bed and turned on the light. Across the room, Izma stood, watching her.

"Take the silver from elsewhere," she said.

Izma shook his head. "We have a bargain."

"Forget the bargain," Karen said. "I don't want anything else."

"It is too late to change our bargain."

Karen held her hand on the chain that was slowly growing shorter, one tiny bit of silver at a time, slowly closing around her neck. Already, even though the necklace was not yet tight, she found herself struggling to breathe. Karen fingered the clasp.

"Tell me what will happen if I remove this," she said.

His eyes gleaming in anticipation, Izma told her.

Karen shuddered. Then she screamed.

ALEXANDER WATCHES
A PLAY

Alexander would much rather have gone to a movie or just stayed at home and watched television. But his mother had bought a ticket to the new production at the Sommerset Children's Theater, and she was the sort of mom who would never let anything go to waste. So Alexander knew there was no way out.

"What's it about?" he asked as his mother dropped him off in front of the building.

She handed him the ticket. "I don't know. It doesn't say. You'll find out. I'm sure it will be wonderful."

"Right." Alexander gave his ticket to a man at the door, then headed into the lobby. He looked around. There were no signs or posters. No popcorn, either.

Alexander stepped inside and found his seat. It was in the front row. A moment later, the man who'd taken his ticket walked out from behind the curtains. "Welcome," he said. "It's my pleasure to introduce our final production of the season. So sit back and enjoy yourself while the Sommerset Children's Theater presents the world premiere of *Alexander Watches a Play*."

Alexander sat up in his seat at the sound of his own name. The curtain opened. On the stage, a boy and his mother were sitting on wooden chairs inside a cardboard box painted to look like a car.

"What's it about?" the boy onstage asked.

He wasn't a very good actor, Alexander thought. *I could do better than that. Not that I'd ever want to be in a stupid play.*

Onstage, the boy's mother answered. She didn't seem to be a very good actor, either. They talked for a moment; then the boy walked through a door. The curtain closed.

What in the world . . . ? Alexander wondered.

The curtain opened. The stage had a row of theater seats. The boy onstage was watching another stage. A man walked out in front of the curtains of the new stage. "Welcome. It's my pleasure to introduce our final production of the season."

The man introduced the play. The curtain behind him opened. Alexander watched as the boy onstage watched another boy who was sitting in box painted to look like a car.

This can't go on, Alexander thought.

But it did. He watched a play about a boy named Alexander who watched a play about a boy who watched a play, and on and on. The theater seemed to get endlessly deeper as each new version started. Alexander thought about getting up and leaving, but he was curious to know how long the play could keep going. After a while, the actors were so far away that Alexander could barely make them out. He had to strain to hear what they were saying.

Then, far off, he heard an actor cry, "Oh no, the balcony is falling."

There was a crash. Another voice cried out, "The poor boy. He's been crushed."

The farthest curtain closed. Once again, Alexander heard: "Oh no, the balcony is falling," followed by another slightly louder crash.

Theater by theater, the crash came closer. Soon it was on the stage right in front of Alexander. A man on the stage shouted, "Oh no, the balcony is falling." Then the Alexander onstage shot up from his seat and turned around. But instead of running, he froze.

"Stupid kid," Alexander muttered. This was just too unrealistic, like one of those hokey wrestling matches where one guy is lying there, acting too stunned to get up, and the other guy takes forever to make his next move.

"Run, you idiot!" Alexander shouted. He watched as the balcony onstage fell right on top of the actor playing Alexander. It seemed to move in slow motion—groaning and creaking for a while and then finally toppling. As the curtain closed, Alexander looked up. The theater's balcony was right over his head. A strange groan came from above.

A man at the end of Alexander's aisle shouted, "Oh no, the balcony is falling."

I'm outta here! Alexander knew he had plenty of time

to reach the exit before the balcony fell. He shot from his seat and turned around, planning to make a dash for the exit. Instead, Alexander froze, stunned by what lay in front of him. His row of seats was on a stage. He squinted into the lights, then looked out at the people in the audience. That alone wouldn't have been quite enough to keep him frozen. But beyond the theater, he saw another, and another, and another, stretching away forever.

"Stupid kid," a boy muttered from darkness.

The boy shouted something else, but the words were drowned out in the crash and clatter of the collapsing balcony.

MR*S*. BARUNKI

I hate Mrs. Barunki. She's the worst teacher in the school. I can't believe I got stuck with her for second grade. When I found out, I almost ran away from home. The worst part is that I came so close to not getting her. If I was one year younger, I'd have been safe. She's retiring at the end of this year. That's just about all she talks about. That and her stupid math facts. She makes us memorize stuff every single day. I'm sick of it. She makes us learn lots more math than we'll ever need.

But we get her back. All the kids hate her. We play tricks on her whenever we can. It's war—us against her. She teaches us math facts, we hide all her pencils. She teaches us math facts, we make faces when she turns away.

She used to shout a lot. That's what I heard from some of the older kids. This year, she hasn't shouted at all. But I still hate her. And she hates us. I know she does. Mom says that "hate" is a bad word, but Mom doesn't have to sit here every day.

At least the year is almost over. I made it through Mrs. Barunki's class in one piece. I survived.

"Well, boys and girls," Mrs. Barunki said when there was only a minute left on the very last day, "I can't say I'll miss you, and I know you won't miss me. But I'll tell you one thing."

She stopped and grinned at the class, taking time to stare at each and every one of us. When her eyes reached mine, I felt like I was trapped on the wrong side of a cage at the zoo. I waited to see what she would say.

"I'm going away—far away. But you'll never forget me. I can promise you that. I'll be a part of your life forever. I've made sure of that." Then she started laughing.

The bell rang. It was over. I was through with Mrs. Barunki and her meanness and her math facts. She couldn't do anything more to me.

And she was wrong. No matter what she said, I knew I wouldn't ever think of her again. As sure as the sky is blue, as sure as water is wet, and as sure as two times three is seven, Mrs. Barunki was out of my life for good.

MURGOPANA

The old man held a large rock in his left hand and spoke a single word. He reached down with his right hand and grabbed a fistful of sand from the beach. Brendan, sitting on a fallen tree several yards away, watched as his father tried to find meaning in the strange sounds.

"*Shanbruk,*" the man said lifting the rock higher.

"*Shanbruk,*" Brendan's father said, writing the word in his notebook.

The old man grinned. Brendan noticed that he had lost most of his teeth. Holding out his palm with the small mound of sand, the old man said, "*Shanpana.*"

Brendan got up, walked barefoot across the warm sand, and stepped into the gentle surf that rippled against the north edge of this small island in the Pacific. "I'm going out for a swim," he called to his father.

Brendan's father gave him an absentminded wave. "Have fun."

"I will." Brendan waded away from shore until he was

waist deep in the water, then leaned back and floated. *This is the life*, he thought. Even if his dad's work was kind of silly, Brendan was enjoying his time on Senshoji Island. He just wished things would get a little more exciting once in a while. Even paradise could get boring.

Brendan drifted around and looked over toward the shore. His father was still talking to the old man, collecting more words. The people on the island—they called themselves the Wanoshenu—spoke a language that wasn't used anywhere else. It wasn't even all that much like any other known language. As far as Brendan could tell, people who cared about languages, people like his father, went wild over the chance to study a new one. It was sort of like when an astronomer finds a new star or a biologist discovers an unknown animal.

"I'll be staying with them for a month," Brendan's father had explained. "I have to compile a lexicon—that's a list of the words in the language. Then I can start studying the grammar. I've made arrangements for you to come with me, if you'd like."

It sounded pretty boring to Brendan. At least, it had sounded boring at first, but then he'd remembered something he'd learned in school. He'd thought about those twenty-four dollars' worth of beads and trinkets and how, if he remembered correctly, Peter Someone-or-other had bought Manhattan Island that way. *What could I buy with some shiny junk?* Brendan wondered.

"I'd love to go," Brendan told his dad. Then he headed into town, where he'd picked up a nice assortment of fake jewelry, sparkly beads, and other glittery products of a plastic civilization.

The islanders had gone crazy over the stuff—especially the rhinestones. It would have been perfect if they'd had anything good to trade. But they didn't have lots of knives or spears or anything cool. They had baskets and clothing. Brendan didn't need baskets, and he definitely didn't want their used clothing. So he was stuck on Senshoji Island for a month with nothing to do but swim and lie on the beach.

It could be worse, he thought, as he drifted with the rolling waves. The water was warm, the sun was warmer, and his dad let him sleep as late as he wanted. An hour later, when Brendan waded back onto the beach, he saw that his father was just finishing up the interview with the old man.

"Brendan, this is fascinating. Come have a look," his father said, waving his notebook. He reached down to switch off the tape recorder.

"Sure," Brendan said, though he wasn't the least bit interested. He joined his father and looked at the notebook. As his father talked about phonemes, morphemes, and rounded vowels, Brendan nodded and grunted, but he really wasn't paying any attention. The whole thing was boring.

When his father was finished, they walked back toward their tent. On the way, they stopped to stare at the stone statue that stood in a clearing on the path. The natives referred to it as *Murgobruk*. But to Brendan, it might as well have been called Bug-Fish. It was a huge statue, towering at least twenty feet in the air, that looked like a combination of a cockroach, a fish, and a lobster. The thing that always caught Brendan's eyes was the mouth, with a pair of jaws lined with sharp teeth made of carved white shells. A fin with spiny bristles ran along the creature's back. It had five pairs of jointed legs. The front pair ended with claws. Its body terminated in a forked tail that was covered with spikes.

"I'd hate to run into one of those," Brendan's father said. "Not that such a thing could exist. Anything that size would be crushed under its own weight."

"That's a relief," Brendan said. He didn't think a creature like the *murgobruk* could exist, but the huge statue still gave him the creeps. *A little one would be fun*, he thought. Maybe he could get one of the natives to carve a small model for him to take home. Not that there was any way he could communicate his request.

"Real or not," his father said, "it's certainly fascinating to observe the beliefs of an ancient culture from such a close vantage point. Imagine how much we'll be able to learn once we know the basic language."

He said more, but Brendan had tuned him out again. They reached their tent, which was set up next to the Wanoshenu village. Brendan saw some of the kids his age playing a game with small stones. He wandered over and watched for a minute. Remembering the word the old man on the beach had used, Brendan pointed at the stone and said, "*Shanbruk?*"

The boy looked at him and laughed. Then he said, "*Naybu.*"

That was one of the few words Brendan knew. It meant "no." He tried again. "*Shanpana?*"

"*Naybu, naybu,*" the boy said. He held up the stone. "*Shantoji.*" The word may have been foreign, but the way he said it carried the universal tone of someone patiently trying to educate an idiot.

"Forget it," Brendan said. He went back to the tent and got out his music player. He was going through batteries faster than he'd expected, but he really needed to sit back and blast some tunes.

His father came in a while later. When he started to talk, Brendan removed his headphones.

"Big day tomorrow," his father said. "Some sort of special ceremony."

"Like what?" Brendan asked. That sounded like it might be a nice change of pace.

"I don't know," his father said, "but we'll find out soon enough. I think it has to do with *Murgobruk.*"

Great, Brendan thought, *some kind of bug-fish ceremony.* He put his headphones back on and listened to music until he felt sleepy.

The next morning, Brendan was startled awake by shouting. A boy named Jasi stuck his head in the tent and yelled, "*Murgopana! Tanu gan weroba! Murgopana!*"

Brendan shot off of his cot, wondering what was going on. He staggered outside, along with his father. The villagers were all heading toward the mountain that rose from the center of the island.

"What's going on?" Brendan asked his father.

"I don't know, but it will be a great opportunity to learn about these people."

Brendan and his father followed the villagers, who were hustling along the path. The people didn't seemed panicked, but they were definitely tense. From all around, Brendan kept hearing one word: *"Murgopana."*

Once the people reached the inland cliffs, they streamed into a cave. After everyone was inside, they started to drag a large rock across the opening, using wooden handles tied to it with ropes. The village chief looked out toward Brendan and his father. He pointed into the cave and said something.

"Shouldn't we join them?" Brendan asked.

"We won't learn anything in there," his father said. "I'm pretty sure that whatever they're hiding from is going to happen out here." He turned toward the chief and said, *"Naybu."*

The chief touched his chest in a gesture that Brendan knew meant "farewell."

Brendan watched as the boulder sealed the villagers within the cave. "You sure we're safe?"

"Positive," his father said. "They kept mentioning *weroba*. That's the ocean. Whatever is supposed to happen, I think it will happen there." He headed toward the beach.

Brendan followed him. Again, they paused in front of

the statue of Murgobruk. "Why were they shouting, 'Murgopana'?" Brendan asked.

"I'm not sure," his father said. "'Bruk' means 'big'. And 'toji' means 'small.' They attach that to the end of a word. For example, 'horu' is 'man.' So they call me 'horubruk' and they call you 'horutoji.' I'm the big man and you're the little man."

"But what about 'pana'?" Brendan asked when they reached the beach.

His father shook his head. "I haven't quite figured that out yet. It could mean 'tiny.'"

"Well, if the *murgopana* shows up, we'll know the answer," Brendan said. He plunked down on the fallen tree and dug in the sand with his toes. He looked out toward the water. It was unusually calm today. Maybe the natives were afraid of calm water, he thought. That made him grin.

He glanced down at the sand. *Shanpana.* The word bubbled up into his mind. *Shanpana?* Brendan thought back to the day before.

The ocean grew less calm. The water started to churn. Brendan turned toward his father. "'Shanbruk' means 'big rock,' right?"

"Very good," his father said. "And I thought you really weren't interested in my work."

Brendan looked ahead. The water almost seemed to be boiling now. It was frothing and splashing, like a hard rain was pounding it. But the sky was clear. Brendan rose from the fallen tree and took a step toward the ocean. *Shanpana,* he thought. That's what the old guy had called his handful of sand. A handful of sand—many little rocks. *Many little . . .*

Brendan looked at the sand at his feet. Then he looked at the water just ahead of him. The surf practically exploded in a burst of activity. "*Murgopana*," Brendan said, suddenly understanding. Murgobruk was the huge statue. It wasn't real. It was far to big to exist. But *murgopana*, that was different. . . .

Brendan screamed as the *murgopana* burst from the surf and swarmed onto the beach. They looked liked the large statue, but each one was only the size of a scorpion. There seemed to be hundreds of them, maybe thousands. They charged onto the sand in wave after wave. The air filled with the clicking of their claws as they headed toward Brendan and his father.

"*Pana!*" Brendan's father shouted. "I know what it means now."

"I'm way ahead of you, Dad," Brendan said. He turned to run. But the many small creatures, the *murgopana*, had another quality Brendan was about to discover. They were small, but they were also very fast.

EAT YOUR VEGGIES

Eat your spinach," Ed's mother said. She pointed to the mushy green puddle of overcooked goop that quivered on his otherwise-empty plate.

"No way." Ed shook his head. "Why should I?"

"Bad things happen if you don't eat your vegetables," his mother said.

"Yeah, right." Ed took a deep breath. He was not going to eat that spinach, no matter what. Ed pushed back his chair and stood. He took his plate and walked over to the garbage can. Then, watching his mother out of the corner of his eye, he scraped the green glop into the garbage and waited for the explosion.

She didn't say a word. Ed wanted to say, *See, nothing bad happened*, but he knew that he'd be pushing his luck if he spoke. So he just gathered up the garbage bag and took it to the curb, removing even the slightest possibility that he'd have anything more to do with the spinach.

The tall bag fell on its side, but Ed didn't care. As he

walked back toward the house, a mouse came running from underneath the porch. Its keen sense of smell picked up the marvelous aroma of cooked vegetables. The mouse started gnawing at the bag. In seconds, the wonderful spinach gushed onto the ground. Soon several other mice came, drawn by the aroma and the sounds of a feast.

Ed walked into the kitchen, still half-amazed that he'd gotten away with it. He looked over at his mom. She was washing dishes and paying no attention to him.

Down the street, a cat lifted her head, her ears twitching at the sounds and scent of prey. She rose slowly, stretched, and padded along the sidewalk toward the mice. There was no need to slink and stalk. The prey was busy feasting and would never know she was there until it was too late.

Ed put an empty bag in the garbage can. Normally, he would have waited until he was told to do this, but he now saw the can as his partner in the war against vegetables. Future dinners would be so much more pleasant. Ed considered the joys of dumping Brussels sprouts or tossing out lima beans.

Across the street from the Ed's house, a dog spotted the cat and pulled at the rope that held him in his yard. As the dog yanked, the poorly tied rope slipped free. The dog leaped over the fence and started across the road, barking and growling.

Ed went through the kitchen to the living room, ready for the best part of the evening. He sat on the couch and picked up the remote control.

Down the street, a car carrying a man who was coming home from work swerved to avoid hitting the dog. The car hit a utility pole instead. The air bag worked, saving the driver from harm. But the pole broke. It fell, snapping all the wires, including the one that brought cable television into Ed's home.

Ed turned on the television. There was nothing but static. He tried another channel. It was dead. They were all dead. "Hey, Mom," he shouted, "the television isn't working."

"Well," his mother called from the kitchen, "maybe next time you'll eat your vegetables."

INQUIRE WITHIN

This has to be some kind of joke," Quinn said, holding up the current issue of *The Sound Scene*, the local free weekly paper that covered music and entertainment.

"Let me see." Deliah leaned over and read the ad.

TURN IN WITCHES.
MAKE MONEY.
HELP PROTECT SOCIETY.

"It's got to be a joke or something," Deliah said. "It's probably publicity for a play or a movie."

"I don't know." Quinn pointed to the bottom of the ad. "The address is real. Let's go check it out."

Deliah sighed, then got up from the couch. "Whatever." Quinn wasn't her brightest friend. And this would turn out to be something totally stupid. But there was nothing on television and she was bored.

The place was way downtown in a little street filled with junk shops and places selling stuff only tourists would want. There was no name on the window. Just a small sign that read: Inquire Within.

Deliah tried to look inside, but the place was too dark for her to see anything. "It's closed," she said.

Quinn turned the knob. "It's open." She went inside.

Deliah followed her. There was nothing inside except for a table with four chairs. A young woman sat at one of the chairs, drinking tea.

"We want to find out about turning in witches," Quinn said.

Deliah expected the woman to laugh at her or toss them out, but instead, she smiled, pointed to a chair, and said, "Have a seat."

"What's the deal?" Deliah asked as she sat.

"Witches are a threat to us," the woman said. "Tea?"

"No thanks," Quinn said.

The woman's voice sounded normal to Deliah, but her words were crazy. "There are no witches," Deliah said.

The woman shrugged. "Then you can't make any money here."

Quinn glared at Deliah. "Let's say there are witches. What kind of reward do you pay?"

"Five hundred dollars."

When Deliah heard that, it no longer mattered to her whether the woman was crazy. If she was willing to hand out that kind of money, Deliah was willing to play her crazy game. "Do we have to bring the witch here?" Deliah asked. She already had a couple people in mind. Creepy, spooky people who deserved to get in trouble.

"No," the woman said. "Just bring information."

Deliah stood. "Great."

Once they got outside, Quinn asked, "So, how do we find a witch to turn in?"

"We just look for the right signs," Deliah said. "You know—spooky lady who lives alone. Maybe bad things happen to her enemies. Or maybe she never ages."

"Miss Miller!" Quinn shouted, naming their art teacher.

"Right!" Deliah said. "She's got that wart on her chin."

"And remember what happened with Tony Bedner? After he'd made fun of her in class?"

"Oh yeah. That was awful." Deliah had forgotten about that. Tony had fractured his leg the next day, slipping on a perfectly smooth and dry piece of sidewalk. He'd also knocked out three teeth. Even if Miss Miller wasn't really a witch, there might be enough evidence to earn Quinn and Deliah the reward. "Let's go back to my place and make up a list," she said.

By the end of the evening, the girls had come up with nine people who might be witches. They had strong evidence for at least three of them.

"Who'd have thought there were so many witches?" Quinn said.

Deliah nodded. She still didn't really believe in witches, but she had to admit there was a lot of proof that there was something strange about these people. And if Deliah and Quinn got paid for even one of the nine, that would be a lot of money.

"What's going to happen to them?" Quinn asked. "You think they'll get in trouble?"

"That's not our problem." Deliah put the pad away. Then she yawned. "Wow. It's kind of late. I'm pretty sleepy. You mind if we don't watch a movie?"

"That's fine." Quinn got up and headed for the door. "See you tomorrow."

"Yeah. See you tomorrow."

As soon as the door closed, Deliah grabbed the list. It was late, but maybe the place was still open. *I came up with all of this*, she thought. *Or, at least, most of this. So why split the money with Quinn?* Besides, Quinn kept acting like she didn't want to go through with it.

But how to keep Quinn from finding out? Deliah smiled, grabbed her pen, and added Quinn's name to the list. She'd get the money and then, in the morning, tell Quinn she'd changed her mind. Then, if Quinn went by herself, the woman would call her a witch and Quinn would think she was crazy and go away.

"Perfect." Deliah headed out.

The door was unlocked. The woman was there.

"I found some witches," Deliah said.

The woman seemed excited. She pointed to a seat. Deliah sat, then slid the list over to her. The woman spent a minute reading the list. Then she reached under the table and grabbed a metal box. She put it down and flipped open the lid. Deliah gasped as she caught sight of stacks of cash.

"I just need to ask a couple questions about each entry. We have to be sure before we take action. This is a very serious business."

"No problem," Deliah said.

"Tell me about this first one," the woman said. She poured a cup of tea for Deliah.

"She's an art teacher," Deliah said. She described the evidence, then took a sip of tea.

"And the next one?" the woman asked.

Deliah told the woman about her neighbor Ms. Suvaro. She talked for a long time, trying to hold off the moment when she had to make up lies about Quinn. As Deliah finished describing the third person on her list and drained the last of her cup, she asked the one thing that had been bothering her. "Why are you so eager to find witches?"

"We're not," the woman said.

"We?" Deliah asked. She noticed there were people standing near the walls on both sides of her, watching them. But they were hidden in the shadows. The darkness seemed to grow from the walls. The shadows seemed to pulse like they were breathing. And with each breath, they drew closer to her.

"We," the woman said. "We're not trying to find witches."

"Then why . . . ?" Deliah blinked. She was so tired. A nap would be nice.

"We're looking for people who would accuse someone of being a witch," the woman said. She laughed.

But it sounded to Deliah like a cackle. She tried to stand, but her legs had turned to thick, limp ropes. She tried to scream for help, but her tongue had become a useless scrap of cloth.

"We like it here," the woman said. "And we plan to stay. Which means we need to get rid of dangerous, meddlesome people like you."

Deliah was far too sleepy to listen anymore. She rested her head on the table, closed her eyes, and drifted off.

When Quinn reached Deliah's house the next morning, she was surprised to find the police there. Deliah was missing. The police asked Quinn what she and Deliah had done yesterday.

"Watched movies. Talked. That kind of stuff." Quinn couldn't admit they'd thought about doing something as stupid and mean as a witch hunt. It had seemed fun for a moment or two, but last night, as she thought about it, she realized she wasn't the kind of girl to do that to someone. Not that it mattered. Deliah was right. There was no such thing as witches.

THREE

I'm warning you, Dennis, come inside right now," his mother said as she stood by the open front door of their house.

"Just a second," Dennis said without looking up. He was almost finished with the fort he was building for his toy soldiers. He just had to put a few more stones on one side and it would be perfect.

"Now," his mom said.

"Coming." Dennis started to stand up, but he kept placing stones, adding the last of them from a crouching position.

"One," his mother said.

Dennis quickly added the final stone.

"Two."

"All right! I'm coming." Dennis stood and ran up to the porch. That had been close. His mother had almost reached three.

Dennis looked up at his mother and wondered what would have happened if he had let her finish counting.

The next day, he was still thinking about that when he was playing with his friends Lance and Trevor.

"What happens if your mom or dad reaches three?" Dennis asked.

"I don't know," Lance said.

"Your mom ever get to three?" Dennis asked Trevor.

"Nope," Trevor said. "I always tell myself I'm going to ignore her, but then I chicken out when she reaches two."

"Yup, me, too," Lance said.

"I'm going to do it," Dennis said. "I'm going to find out."

"No," Lance said. "It's too dangerous. There's no telling what might happen."

"I don't care. I'm going to find out."

At that moment, Dennis heard the call from down the street. "Dennis. Lunchtime. Come home."

"In a minute, Mom," he called back. Then he sat on the ground and grinned at his friends.

"Dennis, I want you to come right now," his mother called.

"Coming," Dennis said, still sitting and still grinning.

"One."

Dennis sat.

"Two."

Dennis couldn't do it. He leaped to his feet and ran to his house. It was almost as if some force took control of his body. He couldn't fight the power of hearing his mom's count approach three.

He tried again the next day. And yet again the day after that. Each time, no matter how much he told himself he'd fight the call, Dennis was unable to resist the force that made him obey.

"You guys are just going to have to hold me back," he told his friends the next day.

"What?" Lance asked.

"Hold me. When my mom starts counting, I want you to hold me until she reaches three."

"I don't know," Trevor said. "We could all get in trouble."

"Come on," Dennis said. "We have to find out. What's the worst that could happen?"

He kept arguing until his friends finally agreed to help. At dinnertime, when the call came, Dennis sat on the ground. Each of his friends knelt by his side and grabbed an arm.

"One," his mom called.

Dennis sat, not yet feeling any urge to rise.

"Two," his mom called.

Suddenly Dennis panicked. "Let me up," he shouted at his friends. He struggled, trying to break free.

He couldn't get loose.

"THREE!"

The word swept down the street with the force of an ocean wave. Lance and Trevor suddenly let go of Dennis and stepped back. They both stared at him, as if wondering what was going to happen.

Behind him, Dennis heard a door slam. Across the street, he heard another door slam. Suddenly, all up and down the block, doors slammed. People were leaving their houses. Moms and dads were walking out. As Dennis watched, dozens of parents walked from their houses and out into the street. Then they walked away. Without a word, they left.

Dennis saw his mom and dad. He ran after them, but they just kept walking. Finally, Dennis stopped chasing them. He just stood and watched them walk off.

Lance's mom was leaving, too. Trevor's mom and dad were also going. Lance and Trevor turned back toward Dennis.

"It's all your fault," Lance said. "You ruined everything."

"Yeah," Trevor said. "Let's get him."

Dennis took a step back. He opened his mouth to call for help. Then he shut it. There was no one to call, he realized. There was no help.

FAT FACE

I like food. I can't help it. The rest of my life is pretty miserable, but when I'm eating I'm happy. I try to be happy as much as possible. The kids in school call me Fat Face. They call me worse things, too. And they tease me. They'll run up behind me when I'm walking home and poke me real hard. They know I can't catch them. It's a good thing for them I can't run fast. If I caught one of them, I'd pound him until he said he was sorry.

I tried to lose weight. Heck, I tried a hundred times. I just can't stay on a diet.

The worst problem is the older kids. They're too big for me to hit. And they love to torture me. Especially Ronald Volger. He's two years older. He's been kicked out of school five times. He thinks he's so cool because all the girls say he's good-looking. He acts like he's some kind of movie star.

I was walking home from school when Ronald snuck up on me from behind. I was just about to unwrap a

Choco-Squirt bar. It's my favorite. Nice, gooey chocolate, with caramel crème and little hard pieces of that buttery candy. Man, it's good. And after you eat it, the hard pieces stick to your back teeth, so there's something to enjoy for a long time. It's a real mess to eat, though. Not that I mind.

I was so busy thinking about how awesome the bar would taste that I didn't notice Ronald. I didn't even know he was there until he snatched the Choco-Squirt from my hand.

"Got it!" He grinned at me with a face full of perfect teeth and waved my Choco-Squirt in the air. "I got a candy bar. I got a candy bar."

"Give it back," I said. I took a step forward.

"I don't think so." He took a step back.

I took another step. But I didn't get too close. If he turned and ran, I'd never catch him. Why are the bullies always fast and strong? "Come on. It's mine. Give it back."

"Oh, is Fat Face gonna cry? Does Fat Face want his gooey chewy candy?"

"Stop it. . . ."

He reached up and started to tear the wrapper. He kept grinning, giving me the same smile he uses in school to get himself out of trouble with the teachers.

"Don't," I said. I clenched my fists.

"It looks so good, I can't wait." He opened his big mouth and bit down on the Choco-Squirt bar, chomping at it right through the wrapper.

Rage flooded through me, washing away all common sense and caution. Screaming, I charged at him.

He laughed and jogged away. "Mmmm. Yummmm. That tastes good. Thanks for sharing, Fat Face."

I heard him take another chomp. He looked over his shoulder at me as he ran, his face already smeared with chocolate. A ribbon of caramel dripped from the corner of his lip.

"You—," I gasped, unable to say more than that while I chased after him. Blood pounded in my skull. My lungs burned. The muscles in my legs felt as if I'd stabbed them with jagged pieces of glass.

Ronald turned off the sidewalk and jogged through the lot by the old MacKowlan house. Nobody lived there now. Even when the MacKowlans lived there, the place had been a garbage pit. Old refrigerators, broken furniture, and tons of other junk littered the yard.

I weaved my way through the piles of appliances, trying to grab hold of Ronald. I may as well have been trying to grab a shadow. He kept just out of my reach. I knew he was playing—toying with me, getting as much fun as he could from my anger. The smartest thing I could have done was stop chasing him. But I was too angry to be smart.

As he went around the side of the house, he spun toward me and started running backward. That hurt more than the rest of it. Even when he ran backward, I couldn't catch him.

Despite the rage that drove me, I was ready to give up. I was nearly dead from running. My heart was trying to explode. My knees had turned from solid to a thick liquid.

I slowed from a run to a walk and tried to get air into lungs that felt far too small for the job.

Ronald slowed, too, but he kept going backward. Bad move. He backed into a couple of old oil drums. He stumbled over one of them and fell, knocking down more stuff. Scrap piles smashed around him with a sound like a thousand gongs and bells.

When the avalanche stopped, Ronald was lying face-down, pinned flat on the ground. I felt the drum that was across his legs. It was probably heavier than I could move.

He let out a stream of swearwords. Then he said, "Help me."

He tried to look at me, but there was a hunk of steel beam across the back of his neck, so he couldn't even turn his head. I noticed the remains of the Choco-Squirt in his fist. I saw the smears of chocolate and caramel on his face. I noticed something else.

"I'll get help," I said.

"Hurry," he said.

"I will." I couldn't stop staring at the ground.

"Get moving, you fat blimp."

"Sure. I'll go as fast as I can," I told him. I walked a few steps away, then paused. I was still out of breath. I took a few more steps. I guess I could have gone faster, but I was tired. And I kept stopping to think about what I'd seen.

Behind me, I heard the first startled shout from Ronald. It wasn't very loud. The next cry was a bit louder. I moved farther away, not wanting to be near when the real screaming started.

I stopped again to catch my breath and closed my eyes. In my mind, I could see his face, covered with chocolate and caramel, pushed flat against the ground. His face was right next to dozens of little piles of dirt—the sort of piles any kid recognizes instantly. Anthills. Red ants. The kind with a bite that feels like fire.

As the screams grew louder, I walked around the house and headed toward the street. I did say I'd get help for him. And I would. I just wasn't in any hurry. My face might be fat, but at least I had a face. As I walked, I reached into my pocket for another Choco-Squirt. But when I saw Ronald's face again in my mind—saw it as it was becoming—my hand dropped to my side. I realized I wasn't all that interested in eating anything right now. Maybe, this time, if I held on to that image, I'd finally be able to stick to a diet.

THE SODA FOUNTAIN

Ben always paused for just a moment before he went into Mr. Paulson's shop. That was one of the ways he made the whole experience last longer. He felt that Saturday afternoon really started when he put his hand against the frosted glass of the door and it ended when he stepped back outside. That span of time in between, well, that was certainly the best part of the day and absolutely the best part of the week.

Ben knew there weren't a lot of soda shops left. There were other places where a kid could get a soda made from syrup and seltzer, but there weren't many spots where a kid could really sit, enjoy his soda, and take his time. But as long as there was Paulson's Sweet Shop, Ben was happy.

Ben pushed the door open. The soda fountain was at the back of the small shop. Ben walked between two rows of magazine racks, looking for anything new that might have come in. Nothing caught his eye. The lingering aroma of bacon drifted through the air. Mr. Paulson didn't just make sodas—he also cooked breakfast on the weekends. But Ben wasn't interested in bacon and eggs.

"Hey, here comes my favorite customer," Mr. Paulson said. He was standing behind the counter with a rag in his hand. He always had a cloth ready for wiping up spills.

"Hi," Ben said, climbing up on the stool. He spun around, once to the left, then once to the right.

"So, what can I make for you today?"

That was the question. Ben never knew ahead of time what he would order. There were so many choices. That was one of the wonders of syrups—they could be combined. He could get a cola, or a cherry cola, or a chocolate soda, or chocolate cherry, or about half a zillion other flavors.

"Cherry vanilla," Ben said, suddenly realizing what he wanted.

Mr. Paulson nodded. "Good choice. Coming right up." He took a paper cup and squirted it with streams of thick syrup from two of the pumps on the counter. Then he grabbed a hose and sprayed seltzer into the syrup. "Cherry vaaaannnnnilllla," he said, giving Ben a smile as he placed the cup in front of him.

"Thanks." A cluster of straws stood in a glass container on the counter. Ben selected one, peeled off the wrapper—resisting the urge to shoot the paper across the room—and put the straw in the soda.

It was heaven. That first cold, amazing sip was always the best. The rest was great, but there was nothing like the first tingling taste—sweet, cold, and bubbly. Ben spun around again on the stool. There was nobody else in the store. There never was. Sometimes Ben wondered how Mr. Paulson stayed in business. But the store was always there, waiting for him.

Mr. Paulson wiped the counter with his rag. Ben took a long, slow sip. They were separated by years in age, but they were like two old friends, comfortable with their routine.

Behind Mr. Paulson, the grill sputtered and flared up. He barely glanced over his shoulder, then shrugged. "Guess I'd better get that old thing fixed one of these days."

"Guess you'd better," Ben said, smiling. He'd heard that before.

Finally, no matter how slowly Ben sipped, he reached that last noisy slurp. "Thanks," he said, putting his money on the counter. He pushed the cup forward and got off the stool, spinning around once more for the pleasure of it.

"Come again," Mr. Paulson said.

"I sure will." Ben retraced his path to the door. As he stepped outside, the light hurt his eyes for a moment. When he could see clearly again, he noticed a little girl and her mother walking up the street. The girl ran ahead of her mother.

"My name's Brandy," she said. "What's your name?"

"Ben Jensen."

"What were you doing in *there?*" she asked.

"Getting a soda. I always get a soda on Saturday," Ben said.

"You must be crazy." She backed away from him. "Mr. Paulson died two years ago when the sweet shop burned down."

Ben opened his mouth but couldn't think of a reply. There really wasn't anything worth saying to someone as silly as this girl.

The mother grabbed her daughter's hand. "Who are you talking to?" she asked.

"To Ben Jensen," the girl said.

"Young lady," her mother said, "you know better than to say such things. Ben died two years ago when the sweet shop burned down. What would people think if they heard you talking like that?" She led her daughter quickly down the street.

Ben watched them go. He wondered why the woman would say such a ridiculous thing. But that didn't matter. What mattered was that it was time for his soda. He turned to the door of Paulson's Sweet Shop, pausing for a moment to make the experience last longer. Some things were just too wonderful to rush.

SNIFFLES

So I sniff a little once in a while. Everybody does. But Mom is the kind of parent who slaps a Band-Aid on every scratch and considers a chest cold an occasion for extreme medical measures.

In other words, for Mom, my sniffling was reason to go to a doctor. But not any doctor. Mom was taking me to see an allergist. I knew what that meant. My friend Gilbert had allergies. He got a shot every week. There was no way I was putting up with that. Even with the shots, Gilbert was a mess. He stayed away from any place that had cats, dogs, birds, or rodents. He avoided all kinds of foods. He wouldn't even come over to my house after he spotted a tiny bit of poison ivy growing on the side of one tree.

"This is completely unnecessary," I told Mom as she pulled into the parking lot. I didn't hear her answer. My attention was snagged by a totally awesome car. It looked like one of those sports cars they only make ten of a year. Maybe a custom-built Lamborghini or Maserati or something. The license plate said SNEEZDR. Sneeze Dr. Very funny. I guess SNOTMAN was already taken.

We went to the waiting room and took a seat. All too soon, a nurse popped her head in and said, "Norman?" The way she was smiling, I knew I was going to suffer some serious pain.

I followed her down a hall into an examination room. She took my blood pressure, then patted my head and said, "What a good boy you are."

I wondered whether I should bark or maybe tell her what a good nurse she was.

"Dr. Grande will be right with you," she said.

Sure enough, Dr. Grande came in a minute later, carrying a clipboard.

"So . . . ," he stopped and glanced at his clipboard, ". . . Norman, you have allergies."

"Not really," I said, catching myself in midsniffle.

"It's nothing to be ashamed of. Allergies are very common. But I can help. Where do you go to school?"

I told him.

"Do you play sports?"

"Soccer," I said. "And basketball."

"Do you have a lot of friends?"

"I'm pretty popular."

"Relatives?"

"A bunch. What's this have to do with allergies?" I was dying for one good sniffle, but there was no way I was going to do that in front of him. I was still hoping to prove I didn't have any allergies.

"I'm just getting a sense of how many people you come in contact with," he said.

I looked over at the counter that ran along two of the walls. It had dozens of small bottles on it. "Are you going to test me?" That's the worst thing Gilbert told me about. The doctor scratched his arm with all this different stuff to see what he was allergic to. He told me his arm puffed up like a marshmallow in the microwave.

Dr. Grande shook his head. "No. I don't think that's necessary in your case. One shot should do the trick." He unlocked a cabinet and removed a small bottle.

"Just one?" Normally, I'd fight against even that, but after figuring I'd be jabbed a zillion times getting tested for everything from pollen to cat dander and then shot up with allergy stuff each week, I wasn't going to complain.

The shot didn't even hurt. "It should kick in by tomorrow," Dr. Grande said.

"Nice car," I said as I got out of my chair.

"It's my one luxury," he said.

I went back to the waiting room. Mom was happy that I'd been cured, until she wrote out the check to pay for my visit. I was happy the whole thing was over.

Sure enough, the next morning I wasn't sniffling at all. But Mom was. So was everyone on my bus. When I got to school, Gilbert ran up to me, started to say something, then sneezed so hard, I thought he'd snap his neck. I ducked, but I wasn't fast enough to avoid all of the spray.

"Oh, man," he said after he wiped his nose with the

handkerchief he always carried. "Must be a high pollen count or something. I'd been doing so well."

"I got one shot and I'm fine," I said, wiping my face.

"No way. Who's your doctor?"

"Dr. Grande."

"My mom says he's real expensive."

I shrugged. I wasn't paying for it. Besides, I only had to go one time, so the cost didn't matter that much. Gilbert sneezed again, but I managed to get out of the way this time.

The kids who sat near me in class were sniffling and sneezing, too. So were my teammates. Both my parents sneezed all through dinner.

The next day, I noticed Gilbert was wearing latex gloves. "What's up with that?" I asked him.

"I'm just trying to isolate myself from allergens," he said. He reached into his backpack and pulled out a box of disposable gloves. "Here. Help yourself. I've got plenty."

I was going to tell him how ridiculous that was, but he was too busy sneezing to listen to me. I did grab some gloves, but only because they make cool water balloons.

I'm not stupid, but it still took me a couple days to figure out what was going on and another day or two to convince myself I wasn't crazy.

Dr. Grande's allergy shot had worked in more ways than one. Thanks to him, people were allergic to me. Anyone I got near started sneezing.

I went into town that day, after school, and waited until he came out of his office.

"Ah, Norton, right?" he said as he took out his car keys.

"Norman."

"Whatever."

"What did you do to me?" I asked.

He tried to look innocent. "I just gave you an allergy shot."

"Right. And now everyone is allergic to me."

He opened his mouth like he was going to deny it. But then he just shrugged and said, "It'll wear off in a couple weeks. You should take it as a compliment."

"What?"

"That formulation is very hard to obtain. I wouldn't waste a shot on someone who isn't popular. You turned out to be an excellent choice. I've already picked up plenty of new appointments." He turned away from me and reached toward the door of his sports car.

"Wait . . . ," I said.

He looked over his shoulder at me. "What?"

"You don't see anything wrong in what you did?" I was hoping for at least some sign that he knew this wasn't right.

"Nothing at all. Are you finished complaining?"

"Yeah. I'm finished."

He grabbed the handle, opened the door, slid onto the seat, and patted the steering wheel. "You're too young to understand how things work. I've got bills to pay."

"It's still wrong." I stepped closer and let out a sneeze. It was obviously a fake one, and pretty childish. It wasn't even very wet, but it was moist enough to do the trick. He wiped his face with his hand, then closed the car door. I watched him drive off.

Maybe he was right. I should feel glad that I'm popular. And glad the shot will wear off. But mostly, I was glad I wore gloves when I rubbed the poison ivy all over the door handle of his car. And I was glad I wasn't Dr. Grande.

SIDEWALK CHALK

At first, Cindy wasn't sure what she'd found. It was smooth and very light. It was round, as wide as a silver dollar, and about five inches long. Best of all, it was pink. She'd discovered it in a corner of the garage behind the box of old sports equipment, buried under some ancient boxes of plant food and spilled bags of fertilizer. She'd been looking for her softball glove, so she and her friend Tracy could play catch.

Cindy stared at the cylinder for a moment and rubbed her finger against it. Her finger came away pink. That's when she realized what it was.

"Hey, sidewalk chalk," she said, holding it up.

"Great," Tracy said. "Let's draw something. We can play catch later."

Cindy shook her head. "I'm a terrible artist." That's why the chalk had gotten shoved in a box. If she tried to draw a square, she got a circle. If she tried to draw a circle, she got a mess.

"Oh, come on. It'll be fun," Tracy said. "Besides, you can't find your glove, so we can't play ball. Let's draw for a while."

Cindy handed the chalk to Tracy. "Sure. Go ahead. You draw. I'll watch."

"I'll start, but you have to draw something," Tracy said.

"I'm a terrible artist," Cindy said again as she followed Tracy out of the garage.

"That doesn't matter," Tracy said. She knelt on the driveway and drew a flower. Then she drew a fish.

"Wow, you're really good," Cindy said.

"Here," Tracy said, handing her the chalk. "You try."

"I told you I'm not good," Cindy said.

"Just try."

"You're always making me do things I'm not good at," Cindy said.

"That's what friends are for."

Cindy sighed, took the chalk, and started to draw. She figured that if she drew something really big, maybe it would come out better. Since she loved dogs, she decided to draw a puppy. As she was finishing the drawing, she noticed a wonderful fragrance. She looked at the driveway, in front of Tracy. There was a flower there.

"Your drawing," she said to Tracy. Before she could say anything more, she was interrupted by the sound of a frantically flopping fish.

"It's all turning real," Tracy said, taking a step back.

"That's perfect." Cindy noticed that her drawing was

taking form, too. It was starting to become solid. That was great. She'd always wanted a puppy.

"Why'd you draw that?" Tracy asked.

"Why not?" Cindy didn't understand why Tracy looked so pale. "Are you afraid of dogs?"

"Dogs? Are you crazy? It's a dinosaur. Run!"

"Come on," Cindy said. "I drew a puppy." She looked at the thing forming on the driveway. "Oh no. . . ."

Tracy was right. It was a dinosaur. As the head lifted from the driveway, it snapped up the fish and swallowed it whole. Then it looked at the girls.

"I told you I was a lousy artist," Cindy said as she tossed the chalk aside and followed her friend at full speed down the driveway.

"Run!" Tracy screamed.

For once, Cindy totally agreed with her friend. Running seemed like a great idea. A much better idea than drawing.

DON'T EVER LET IT
TOUCH THE GROUND

Careful," I told my little brother, Felix, when I saw him marching up and down the front yard with the flag. He had the pole on his shoulder, but he was so short that one corner of the flag hung just a couple of inches from the ground.

"Careful about what?" he asked.

"You're almost letting it drag." I didn't even know if he was allowed to take the flag out of the house or even touch it. Dad kept it in the closet and only put it out on flag-flying holidays.

"So?"

"You're not supposed to let it touch the ground. Everyone knows that." *At least, everyone but stupid little brothers,* I thought.

"Why not?" he asked.

That's the problem with Felix. He doesn't accept what I tell him. He's always asking for explanations. "Because," I told him.

"What? Just because? That's not an answer."

"Well, you could get arrested."

He shook his head. "You're making it up. I don't be-lieve you. Watch this." He swung the pole off his shoul-der and brought the flag in front of himself. His thin arms were shaking as he struggled against the weight.

"Stop messing around," I warned him.

"I'm gonna do it."

"I told you to stop."

"Here goes," he said. He lowered the flag until it was just above the grass.

"Felix, don't do it. Don't ever let it touch the ground."

He grinned at me and let the pole drop another inch. A corner of the flag rested on the grass. "Oh no, I'm go-ing to get arrested. I'm a criminal."

I rushed over and snatched the pole from his hands, raising the flag high off the ground.

"Hey!" he said. "Give it back. I'm telling."

"And I'll tell on you," I said. "Then you'll be in big trouble." I carried the flag inside. Behind me, through the closing door, I could hear Felix shouting. He was calling me some pretty nasty names. Felix has a bad temper. But no matter what, he shouldn't have let the flag touch the ground. I know that. I mean, I don't know if there's a law or anything. But that doesn't matter. He just shouldn't have done it. There are some things you just don't ever do, like hit a girl or tell on a friend.

I put the flag in the closet. But instead of standing it in its usual spot, I untied it from the pole and hid it up on the shelf behind Dad's old hats. Felix would never find it there.

I didn't think any more about it that day. Felix wouldn't tell Mom or Dad, of course, because I would have told them what he'd done. And Dad would have spanked him, because Dad's pretty patriotic. So Felix knew enough to keep his mouth shut. And I'll bet he knew I was right, too. You never let the flag touch the ground.

That night, after I'd gone to bed, I started thinking about the flag again. Felix was already sleeping. He got up way too early most of the time and usually crashed pretty soon after dinner. I could hear him breathing—slowly and deeply—in his bed over by the opposite wall.

Someone had to teach him a lesson.

He'd let the flag touch the ground. That wasn't right. Nobody else knew, so it was up to me. I'd show him. As a big brother, that was part of my job. My favorite part. I couldn't help smiling as I slipped silently out of bed. At first, I thought I'd just sneak over and shout something to scare him. *It touched the ground!* Or maybe just, *Protect the flag!* But that wasn't enough to teach him a real lesson. It had to be better. I wanted him to remember what I taught him forever.

I went downstairs and got the flag from the closet. I was very careful not to let it touch the ground when I carried it back up the stairs. Right outside the room, I draped it over my head and shoulders. I wanted to look like Death does in the cartoons, with his hood flapping over his face, hiding his eyes. That would scare Felix. I realized

I could hold a flashlight under my chin to make myself look even spookier. I'd wake him and pretend I was coming to take him away.

As soon as he started screaming, I'd dive into bed and hide the flag under the covers. Then, when the folks came, I could tell them Felix was having a nightmare.

That would teach him. Maybe he'd be so scared he'd even confess what he'd done.

I grabbed the flashlight that I kept in my desk and walked to the side of Felix's bed. He looked so peaceful, I almost didn't wake him. But he had to be taught a lesson. And I was willing to do it. It's like Dad always said—this was for his own good.

I reached toward his shoulder.

"Which one?"

The whisper, from behind me, was so soft I thought it was just some stray echo of my own thoughts.

"Isn't it obvious?"

The second voice was louder. I spun. And froze.

Two men stood across the room, dressed in tattered uniforms from the Revolutionary War. I could see the wall through them.

"Him," the man on the left said, pointing at me. "He mocks the flag we died for."

I shook my head. *Not me*, I wanted to scream. But fear had gripped my throat.

"He wears the flag we bled for, as if it was no more than a cast-off blanket." The second man stepped toward me.

"It was bad enough that he let it touch the ground. But we can't allow this mockery to continue."

"Not me." This time I got the words out. "Him," I said, pointing to Felix. "He let it touch the ground."

"No honor," the first man said. "See how he accuses others? He's a liar, and a coward as well."

He stepped closer, reached out, and touched my face. His fingers, cold as a marble headstone in winter, clutched my jaw. He pulled my face forward and put his own face less than an inch away. When he spoke, I felt no breath. No heat. Just the cold, damp smell of the grave. "Never let it touch the ground."

The second man put his face close to mine, too. Nothing reflected from his dry eyes. I couldn't even see my own fear.

"Never let it touch the ground," he said.

"Never let it touch the ground," they both said, pushing me backward toward the wall.

It wasn't me. That's what I wanted to say. They had to understand. But that's not what I said. I knew those words would anger them. I nodded; even that motion was hard. My head wanted to tremble in every direction. "Yes. I'll never let it happen again. I swear."

For a moment, the first man squeezed my jaw so hard I thought the bones would crack. Then he stepped away from me. "Never," he warned.

"Never," warned the second man.

They backed away. Then, still moving backward, they passed through the wall of my room.

My heart was slamming against my ribs so hard, I was afraid it would burst out of my chest. As soon as I could move, I took the flag from my shoulders and folded it—carefully. I was too scared to take it back through the dark hallways to the closet downstairs, so I put it on my desk.

Then I crawled under my covers, closed my eyes, and shivered until I fell asleep.

In the morning, I shot up from my bed as the images of the two ghosts tore into my dreams. Their voices, like wind in dry corn husks, clawed at my mind.

Don't ever let it touch the ground.

There was no flag on the desk.

A dream . . . ?

It had to be. I took a deep breath and tried to calm down. It was just a bad dream. That explained everything. There aren't any vengeful ghosts bringing doom to anyone who allowed the flag to touch the ground. Vengeful and capable of making mistakes.

Surely not.

I looked across the room.

Felix wasn't in his bed. No surprise. He liked to get up early.

I rose and stretched. My pleasure was brief. A feeling of unease settled on me. Faintly, from far off, I heard singing. At first, I couldn't make out the words. But I recognized the rhythm. ONE, two, THREE, four. Then, as the singer moved closer, I heard the words.

"Over hill, over dale, we will march the dusty trail . . ."

A marching song. A song for walking and carrying a

flag. I ran to the window. Below, in the front yard, Felix paraded with the flag over his shoulder. The flag he'd taken from the desk. Not from the closet where I'd hidden it. From the desk—where I'd thought I'd put it in a dream.

No dream. The men were real. I touched my jaw. My flesh burned with the memory of those frozen fingers.

Felix marched across the lawn with the flag he'd taken from the desk. The flag that had scraped the ground with one striped corner, sending a call to the night visitors.

He'd let it touch the ground.

They'd be back tonight. I knew that now. But not for Felix. They'd be back for me.

PICKING UP

John started with the clothes. That was the easiest part. It was a simple matter of sorting things. He put the dirty ones in the hamper. Then he folded the clean ones and put them in his dresser. The ones that might have been clean and might have been dirty also got tossed in the hamper, just to be sure. "I wonder how my room got this messy so quickly," he said.

He looked around the room. There was a bit more floor space now, with the clothes taken care of. But that still left the scattered piles of toys, games, movies, and books.

"This is going to take all day," he said as he started shelving the books.

There wasn't enough room for all of them. He put the older ones, including all the picture books, in a box and took it downstairs. It was funny—he didn't remember reading any of the picture books, but he knew he must have. They were worn and some of them looked like they'd been read hundreds of times.

He went back upstairs and started on the closet. That was the strangest part. As he sorted and stacked and straightened, he realized that, beneath the top layer of familiar possessions, he didn't recognize a lot of the stuff. But it didn't matter. He knew he needed to straighten up. That was the most important thing.

As John put the last game in its place, two boys walked into the room.

"Oh good, you're done," the taller boy said. He turned to the other boy. "Great model for stuff like picking up," he told him. "But not much memory. I'm saving up for an expansion module. I figure I can get him another couple gigabytes someday."

He reached over and touched something on John's chest.

The world went away.

The world came back.

John started with the clothes. That was the easiest part. It was a simple matter of sorting things. He put the dirty ones in the hamper. Then he folded the clean ones and put them in his dresser. The ones that might have been clean and might have been dirty also got tossed in the hamper, just to be sure. He knew he needed to straighten up. That was the most important thing. Sometimes, he felt it was the only thing.

HEAD OF THE CLASS

Please, Rusty thought as he waited for Mrs. Grimkin to return his paper, *let it be okay this time*. But he knew from the angry sound of her steps as she approached his desk that his paper was not anywhere near okay.

"Well, Rusty," Mrs. Grimkin said, holding the paper as if it were coated with a thick layer of wet germs, "you didn't do very well." She dropped the report on his desk and turned toward her next victim.

Rusty stared at the page—a sea of red circles and lines highlighted his mistakes. "Stupid assignment," he muttered. *Who cares about spelling and grammar? So what if I misspelled a few words?* If he wrote "lite" where he should have written "light," anyone reading it would still know what he meant. No matter what anybody said, Rusty knew that spelling wasn't important. Especially not tiny mistakes like the ones his teacher loved to point out.

As Rusty watched Mrs. Grimkin walk toward the front

of the class, rage filled him, pumping into his heart and lungs and gut. He wanted to shout at her. But he'd already been kept after school more times than anyone else in the class. Instead of shouting, he closed his eyes and spoke softly, trying to hold in the anger. "I wish whatever I did was right. I wish I made the rules."

He almost managed to calm down. But when he opened his eyes and saw the paper again, the anger exploded. He crumpled the sheet, squeezing it with all his strength into a tight ball. Leaping to his feet, he launched the paper across the room, not aiming anywhere, just trying to fling his rage away. The wadded paper shot toward Mrs. Grimkin, hurtling straight for the back of her head as she reached her desk.

Rusty froze, his arm still extended.

Mrs. Grimkin bent to pick up a book.

The paper zipped past her head, just brushing the top fringes of her hair. It struck the blackboard and bounced up, following a perfect arc until it landed with barely a rustle in the half-filled wastebasket.

As Mrs. Grimkin rose with the book in her hand and turned to face the class, Rusty realized he was still standing. He sat quickly.

"Man, are you lucky," Steve said, leaning toward Rusty from his desk in the next row. "That was a million-to-one shot. Maybe a zillion to one. She'd have kept you after school for the rest of the year if you'd hit her. Maybe even gotten you expelled for good."

Rusty nodded. He felt incredibly lucky. But the luck

didn't last long. It vanished completely when Mrs. Grimkin said, "Clear your desks, class. Time for the spelling test."

Test? Rusty grabbed his spelling book. "I forgot to study," he said.

"You're doomed," Steve said. "This is a hard one."

Frantically, Rusty flipped the book open. *What chapter was it?* Rusty looked at the page. No, those words seemed too familiar. They'd already done them. He flipped more pages but went too far. Those words weren't right at all. Sweat rolled down the back of Rusty's neck. He continued to search through the book. Finally, he found the page with this week's words.

"CLEAR YOUR DESKS, CLASS!"

Rusty almost toppled off his chair as the shout crashed through his brain. Mrs. Grimkin was standing directly over him, glaring down with the undeniable danger of a stick of dynamite with just a billionth of an inch left on the fuse. Feeling that doom was about to grab him and squash him no matter what he did, Rusty shut his book and jammed it in his desk.

"Stupid spelling," he muttered as he took out a piece of paper.

"Barrel," Mrs. Grimkin said, giving the first word.

Rusty muttered several phrases that would never be on any spelling test. Why did they have to start with that word? He could never remember whether it was "barrel" or "barrle."

"Holiday," Mrs. Grimkin said, spitting out the happy word like it hurt her mouth.

Quickly Rusty wrote "b-a-r-r-e-l." It didn't look right. He erased it and wrote "b-a-r-r-l-e." *That's it*, he thought. He hurried to catch up. His teacher was already on the third word.

Rusty knew, as he handed in his paper, that he was in big trouble. On the way home that afternoon, he saw something that made him stamp his foot against the sidewalk. There, right on the corner of Main and Madison, was a delicatessen called the Pickle Barrel.

"I'm so stupid," Rusty said. He couldn't believe he'd gotten it wrong.

The next morning, first thing, Mrs. Grimkin threaded her way up and down the aisles, handing back the tests. Rusty slunk deeper into his seat, knowing that doom was headed his way. When Mrs. Grimkin reached his desk, she dropped the paper in front of him without saying a word. Rusty stared. His mouth fell open. There, in red ink, where he usually got a 65 or a 70, was a score of 100—a perfect A+ grade. Never in his life had he gotten that high a mark. It had to be a mistake. Or maybe it was a joke. Maybe Mrs. Grimkin would start laughing, then take out her pen, scratch off the grade, and write an F instead.

Rusty scanned the sheet. Right at the top was "barrle." He knew it was wrong. And he knew he should say something. But he didn't.

While Rusty stared at his paper, he heard the tap and skritch of Mrs. Grimkin writing on the chalkboard. Around him, kids groaned. Rusty looked up. It was a history test this time. He hadn't studied. He'd known there was going to be a test, but he'd been too angry last night to open his books. He read the first question.

Who was the fifteenth president?

"Lincoln," Rusty wrote. At least that was an easy one. He went on to the rest of the questions, barely managing to finish before time ran out.

As he left the room at the end of the day, Mrs. Grimkin called to him. "Rusty . . ."

"Yes?" He waited for her to tell him the spelling grade was a mistake.

"It's good to see you finally making an effort," she said.

"Thank you."

Rusty hurried out. On the way home, he almost walked right past the deli without noticing anything. But an odd difference caught his eye. He stared at the sign over the door: The Pickle Barrle.

"But . . ." Rusty ran home and pulled the dictionary from the bookcase. There it was, just like on the sign and on his paper—"barrle."

"I must have forgotten or something," he said, trying to remember exactly what the sign had looked like the day before. Spelling wasn't his best subject, so he knew the dictionary must be right.

Rusty looked up one other thing and found bad news. According to the dictionary, Lincoln was the sixteenth president, not the fifteenth. That meant he had at least one wrong on the history quiz.

Eager to get it over with, Rusty started on his homework. Mrs. Grimkin had told them to write an essay called "What I Do After School." At least he could use the spell-checker on his computer to make sure everything was all right. He'd never bothered using it before. But he didn't want to risk making any more mistakes.

Rusty wrote carefully, trying to be sure there were no errors. The spell-checker caught a bunch of problems but fixed all of them. Once he was sure his essay was perfect, he printed it out. The first copy smeared as it came through the printer. Rusty made a second copy. That one came out fine, though he got a smudge of ink on the back of the page.

The next day, when Rusty turned in his homework, Mrs. Grimkin handed back his history test. Sometimes she let the class read while she graded papers. As the kids around him were taking out their books, Rusty stared at his test. A+. Another perfect score. But what about Lincoln?

Rusty reached into his pocket, pulled out a handful of coins, and grabbed a penny. At least, it looked like a penny. But he didn't recognize the face on the front of the coin. "Who's this?" he whispered, showing the penny to Steve.

Steve gave him a puzzled look. "Grant. Who else? You know, president during the Civil War."

The penny fell from Rusty's fingers and clattered to the floor. *My mistakes become true,* he realized. *But not until Mrs. Grimkin reads them. She must have read the history tests last night.* Suddenly, with shaking hands, Rusty grabbed the smeared copy of his homework.

"Check this, okay?" he asked, shoving it at Steve.

Mrs. Grimkin glanced up, said "Shush," and then went back to grading the homework.

"Kind of late for that, isn't it?" Steve whispered. "You already handed it in."

"Please."

Steve shrugged and took the copy from him.

Rusty held his breath and watched Steve's face for any sign of trouble. A moment later, Steve grinned.

Oh no . . . , Rusty thought.

"You didn't check this very carefully, did you?" Steve asked.

"The computer checked it," Rusty said. "There aren't any mistakes." *There can't be any mistakes.*

Steve shook his head. "No spelling mistakes, but that doesn't mean no mistakes. Here, look." He held out the paper and pointed.

Rusty read the sentence. He didn't see anything wrong. The words were all spelled correctly, as far as he could tell. "It looks fine to me."

"Read it again," Steve said, pointing to the middle of the page.

Rusty read the paragraph. It was about what happened when he got home from school. He'd written: "My mom and dad both work. Some kids have a parent around in the afternoon. I don't have any body." He looked at Steve again, puzzled.

"Right there," Steve said, tapping the words "any body." "That's not what you meant to say. You meant 'anybody.'" Steve smirked, then added, "One word, not two. Big difference."

For an instant, Rusty didn't get it. Then, like the world's largest snowball, the meaning hit him smack in the face. His gaze shot toward the front of the room. Mrs. Grimkin was reading a paper with a smudge of ink on the back. Rusty had to stop her before she read his mistake. He leaped from his seat.

Air whooshed past his ears.

He was falling.

His head hit the desk. Rusty looked down. It wasn't easy. He didn't have any body.

"Good essay," Mrs. Grimkin said, walking up to his desk. She put the paper down, patted Rusty on the head, and walked away.

After a while, the bell rang. The rest of the kids left. Rusty, who didn't have any body, watched them go. A while later, Mrs. Grimkin got up, turned off the light, and went out the door. Rusty, who couldn't head anywhere, just stayed on his desk.

It could be worse, he thought. That was when his nose started to itch.

HALFWAY HOME

Man, that was a long day," Amy said as she walked out the front door of the school. When she reached the corner, she paused and looked down the street in the direction of her house. She could either follow the sidewalk or cut through the new development that was being built in the old field across from the school.

The road was a little hard to walk on in the new section. The workers weren't finished yet, and most of the streets were covered with large pieces of gravel. But it was a lot shorter than going the regular way. Amy decided to cut through the development.

She walked onto the new road that sliced through the side of the field, then turned off on the long road that ran all the way through the development. Amy could follow it to the end, and then she just had to cross the street and walk a half a block to her house.

The road dipped down a little, then rose back up. At

the far end, she could see a stop sign. All around, there were the frames of half-built houses, covered with silver and pink strips of insulation.

As Amy walked, she thought about her day in school. It had been pretty much like any other day, except for that thing her teacher had told them about. Miss Kripke had this period she always set aside for what she called Expanded Horizons. That meant she talked about stuff she thought was interesting, like geology or word origins.

Sometimes it actually was interesting. She'd talked about sports or outer space a couple of times. And once, she'd told them about a guy who'd spent his life carving a sculpture into the side of a mountain. But today it wasn't exciting or interesting. Amy had just found it confusing. As far as she could tell, so did most of the rest of the class.

She looked ahead as she walked. Each step brought her a bit closer to the stop sign.

Closer. That's what Miss Kripke had talked about. Amy tried to remember the name of the thing they'd discussed. Right. It was about some old Greek guy named Zero. No, not Zero. Zeno. Miss Kripke said he'd come up with something called Zeno's paradox. She'd said he proved that motion was impossible.

Amy knew that was stupid. Obviously, things moved. She kicked a rock and watched it skitter across the road. In class, a couple of the kids had pretty much pointed the same thing out. One of the kids in the back row, Sammy Johnson, had even tossed his pencil across the room and shouted, "See that? It moved."

"I know it seems that things can move. But Zeno looked at it differently," Miss Kripke had explained. "To walk from my desk to the wall, I have to get halfway to the wall first. Right?"

"Right," the other kids in the class had said.

"Big yawn," Amy muttered.

"But, before I can go halfway, I have to go half of halfway."

That's when Amy had started to lose track of the concept. Miss Kripke kept talking, explaining the whole thing. It was something about if you kept cutting the distance in half you never ran out of pieces. And if you had to go halfway, first you had to go half of that distance. And so on and so on.

Amy shook her head, as if to get rid of the memory of the class. She looked up. The stop sign seemed closer, but she was surprised she hadn't reached it yet.

She kept going, feeling the sharp edges of the gravel through her sneakers. She walked. She got closer.

But she wasn't getting there.

Amy stopped for a moment. She looked over her shoulder and wondered whether she should just go back the way she'd come. Off in the distance, at the other end of the road, she saw a street sign. But she wasn't sure whether she could ever reach that sign, either.

Amy turned back toward the stop sign and kept walking. As the day grew darker and the sign grew closer, Amy found herself wishing she'd paid more attention in class. She knew, now, that she'd never reach the stop sign. She knew that she'd be walking on this road forever. She only wished she could understand why.

But maybe she could figure it out. She had plenty of time for thinking.

HOP TO IT

Morty almost walked right past the grasshopper. When he first noticed it, he wasn't even sure whether it was an insect or a small stick.

"Hey," he said to Carl. "What's that?" Morty walked over to the side of the road and bent down to take a closer look at the insect.

"It's a cricket or something," Carl said, joining Morty.

"That's not a cricket. It's a grasshopper." Morty was pretty sure crickets were flatter and shaped differently. This was definitely a grasshopper. Not the big green kind but the small brown kind.

"Doesn't matter what it is," Carl said. "It's dead."

Morty bent closer. He was ready to spring back at any moment, just in case the grasshopper tried to jump up at his face. But the insect didn't move. "It's not dead. If it was dead, it would be on its side or something." He took a deep breath and blew on the grasshopper.

It still didn't move.

Morty leaned even closer, looking for any sign of life.

"Dead," Carl said. "Come on. Let's get going."

Morty wasn't sure. He raised his foot and brought it down hard. He smacked the asphalt just behind the grasshopper.

It jumped halfway across the road.

"Cool," Carl said, running over toward it. "My turn." He stomped his foot next to the grasshopper.

It jumped again.

Morty laughed. This was definitely fun. He went over and stomped again. The grasshopper jumped again. "Pretty stupid bug," Morty said.

"Yeah." Carl stomped. His foot almost landed on the grasshopper.

"Careful," Morty said. "You'll squish it."

Carl gave him a disgusted look. "Don't tell me you care about a bug."

Morty shook his head. "I don't care, but if you squish it, we'll have to find another one to play with."

Morty stomped again. The stupid bug jumped again. After Carl stomped, Morty started trying to take two turns in a row.

"Hey, not fair," Carl said.

"I found it," Morty said. "And I figured it out." It was his discovery, so he felt he should have more turns. He stomped. Then he ran to get to the bug before Carl.

The race was on.

Morty was faster than Carl, and he was better at guessing which way the grasshopper was going to jump. So

Morty got to make most of the stomps. But Carl got in plenty, too. They both stomped and pushed and ran until they could hardly breathe.

It was Carl, rushing to try to get in a turn, who made the mistake.

He stomped the grasshopper.

"Carl! You ruined it," Morty said. But he wasn't really angry. He'd been getting tired, and his foot had started to hurt from all the stomping.

"So what? It was just a stupid bug," Carl said. "There are lots of others. The world is full of bugs."

Morty opened his mouth. But he didn't say anything right away. For the first time in a long time, he looked around. He'd been so busy chasing the grasshopper and stomping that he'd paid no attention to where he'd been going. He turned to his left. Nothing looked familiar. He turned to his right. Nothing looked familiar there, either.

"Stupid bug," he said out loud.

"Where are we?" Carl asked.

"I don't know."

They were on a road, but there weren't any houses in sight. There was nothing around them but fields filled with tall weeds. The road itself ended just ahead of them. It came to a sudden stop, as if the people building it had gotten tired and left to do something more interesting.

Carl took a sudden step back from the squished mess that had once been a grasshopper. "I think it led us here," he said.

"That's stupid," Morty said. He didn't like the sound of

panic in Carl's voice. "It was just a stupid bug. And why would a stupid little bug want to bring us here?"

Carl took another step back. "It led us here," he said again. "If someone was chasing you, wouldn't you run somewhere for help?"

Morty couldn't believe Carl would say such ridiculous stuff. But he also felt it was time to find their way home. Something about this place made him nervous. "Let's go."

A shadow fell over him from behind.

Morty turned.

It was another grasshopper. But not a little one. This was a big one. Really big. Bigger than Morty—a lot bigger than Morty.

Morty opened his mouth to scream.

The grasshopper raised one of its front legs. It stomped down. The scream caught in Morty's throat as he saw the bug squish Carl.

The leg came up again.

Stupid bug, Morty thought.

But it was stupid Morty who got squished.

NOTHING LIKE A
HAMMOCK

It was the middle of the summer, and I was bored. My usual friends weren't around today, so I decided to go see Cody Peterson. I hadn't seen him since school let out for the summer, but we'd gotten together at my house a couple of times last year and he was a lot of fun. I knew Cody lived down near the end of Randolph Street. I wasn't sure which house, but I figured it wouldn't be hard to find him. Randolph Street isn't very long.

When I got there, it turned out that most of the houses on Randolph Street had names on the mailboxes. There were only two that didn't, and they were right next to each other.

I checked out the first house. It almost looked like nobody lived there. The windows were shut and the curtains were closed. But I figured it wouldn't do any harm to find out for sure, so I went up the porch and rang the bell.

The door flew open before my finger even left the bell.

"Hello, young lad, what can I do for you?" the man asked. He was tall and thin. Strangely enough, he was wearing sunglasses, which most people don't do when they're inside a house—especially a dark house. As he spoke to me, he kept rubbing his hands together. He was kind of leaning over, too, so his head was almost right above mine.

"I'm looking for Cody. . . ." I expected him to tell me I had the wrong house. He didn't look at all like he was related to Cody.

"Cody's out," the man said. "But he should be returning any second. Why don't you go around back and wait for him."

"I could wait here," I said.

"Nonsense. Go back and relax. Stretch out in the hammock if you want. It's very comfortable. There's nothing like a hammock."

"Sure. Thanks." I walked around the side of the house and went through a gate into the backyard. The yard was surrounded by a fence—a high, solid fence of wood. There wasn't much to see there—no swing set or anything. Just the hammock, which really did look comfortable. It was made of thick ropes stretched out between two trees. What the heck—no reason not to relax while I waited for Cody. And when it came to relaxing, there really was nothing like a hammock.

I knew how to get into a hammock because my uncle

Frank had one at his house up in Maine. I pushed down at the edge and rolled in. My body sank right into the ropes. It felt so nice and relaxing. I closed my eyes.

"I'M HOME!"

I opened my eyes and lifted my head when I heard the shout. That was Cody's voice for sure. But I didn't see him. I heard more shouts. They were coming from the other side of the fence. Then I heard another voice, also on the other side of the fence.

"Cody, wipe your feet before you come in."

"Yes, Mom," Cody said.

I heard a door slam, on the other side of the fence.

The *other* side?

The thought hit me so hard I felt my body jerk. This wasn't Cody's yard. He lived next door. Which meant that the guy I'd talked to wasn't Cody's dad. I needed to get out of here. I started to sit up.

I couldn't.

I was stuck. I tugged and pulled. The outside ropes were fine, but the middle ones, all through the center of the hammock, were sticky, holding me trapped.

I heard another door. This one didn't slam shut. This one creaked open. And it wasn't on the other side of the fence. I looked toward the house. The man slipped out the back door. He dropped to the ground, crawling on his arms and legs. Another pair of legs came out from his sides, through slits in his shirt, and then another. Eight legs. As he crawled toward me, the sunglasses fell from his face, revealing his eyes. They weren't human eyes.

I struggled to break free.

It was no use. I wasn't in a hammock. I was in a web. And even though they might look a little alike, a web is nothing like a hammock.

PUNCTURATION

Connie paused outside the entrance of the shop. There was no reason in the world not to go in. Everyone was doing it. Absolutely everyone in school except her had done it. Most of them had done it years ago. Nearly all of them had done it more than once.

"Well," Nicole asked, "are you going in?"

"Sure," Connie said. She glanced back at her mom, who smiled and nodded. "Why not?" She walked into Peggy's Piercing Palace and looked for a salesperson.

A woman came over. "Can I help you?"

"I'd like to get my ears pierced," Connie said.

"You came to the right place," the woman told her. "Have a seat."

Connie's mom gave her permission, then told the girls, "I'll meet up with you at the food court. Are you sure you don't want me to stay?"

"I'm sure. Thanks." Connie sat and waited while the

woman marked both ears with a red pen. "How's that?" she asked, handing Connie a mirror.

"Great, I guess," Connie said. She looked up at Nicole, who nodded her approval.

"Here we go," the woman said. She leaned over, humming, and put the piercing gun against Connie's right earlobe.

Connie gritted her teeth and waited.

Katchung!

With that, her right ear was pierced.

The pain was sudden and sharp, but it wasn't too bad. *I can take it*, Connie thought. She closed her eyes for a moment as a wave of dizziness hit her. She almost felt like she was falling. But the feeling passed quickly enough. Connie took a deep breath and opened her eyes. She was midway through the ordeal. One more *katchung* and it would be over.

That's when the woman said, "Oops."

"What's wrong?" Connie asked.

"Nothing," the woman said, but she stepped away from Connie, frowning.

"What is it?" Connie asked. She looked at the woman, trying to read her expression. Then she looked at Nicole.

"Oh my gosh," Nicole said. She backed away from Connie, too, but she kept staring at Connie's head. Her eyes were open so wide it looked like her eyebrows were trying to hide under her bangs.

Connie grabbed the mirror and stared at her ear. What

she saw was so unexpected—so plain weird—that she had a hard time making sense of it. Around the pen mark and the tiny post in her ear, something was growing. It looked like the icky white fungus that grows on trees in the woods.

Must have been some crud on the gun, Connie thought. She reached up and brushed at the thing on her ear. Her whole earlobe moved with it. The stuff didn't come off.

She looked back at the woman. "What's going on?"

"Sometimes there's an infection," the woman said. "I'm terribly sorry."

"Fix it," Connie said. "Do something."

The woman shook her head. "I can't."

Connie stared back in the mirror. The fungus was still growing. It spread over her ear and across her neck. She dropped the mirror and grabbed at her ear, wanting to rip the fungus away.

It wouldn't pull free. As Connie removed her hand, she noticed her fingers were covered with the fungus. She tried to scream. But her mouth was covered—sealed by the growth.

She looked at her friend. Nicole was cringing back against the counter, obviously terrified. Connie reached toward Nicole. Then something grew across her eyes. She couldn't see.

She stumbled, trying to find her friend. Seconds later, Connie struggled to breathe through her nose as the fungus spread over the rest of her face.

The world grew dim. Connie felt herself falling to the floor.

She lay in darkness.

All was calm and quiet.

A sharp smell cut through the peace. Connie jolted and tried to turn her head away from the biting odor of ammonia. She heard the woman's voice. "Smelling salts. Works every time."

Then she heard Nicole's voice: "Hey, you okay?"

Connie opened her eyes. She was on the floor. Nicole and the woman were bent over her. "Just stay still, honey," the woman said. "You'll be fine in a minute."

"My ear . . . ," Connie said. She reached up and touched her right earlobe. Something small and cold met her fingers—an earring, just an earring.

"You should have seen yourself," Nicole said. "The second your ear got pierced, you passed out. I tried to catch you, but you dropped right to the floor—just like one of those ladies in the old movies."

"Ready for the other one?" the woman asked.

Ready? Connie wasn't sure. But she didn't think she'd pass out again. She stood slowly and got back on the chair. "Okay. Go ahead."

"Brave girl," the woman said. She leaned over and pierced Connie's other ear, then told her, "All done."

It was over. This time, Connie didn't faint. She paid the woman and left the store. "Glad that's finished," she told Nicole.

Nicole didn't answer. She was staring at Connie's left ear, her face filled with a mix of fear and disgust. She pointed. She opened her mouth.

"What?" Connie asked. She reached toward her ear but was afraid to touch it.

"It's . . ." Nicole paused and swallowed. "It's . . ."

"What?" Connie dug her nails into her palm. The sharp pain told her she hadn't passed out again. Whatever the problem, it was real.

"The hole," Nicole said. "It's not quite centered."

"I can live with that," Connie said. She stopped to look at her reflection in a store window. "It could be worse. It could be a whole lot worse."

THE CHIPPER

Yesterday, I'd sent my soccer ball through the living room window. Today, I was heading to my friend Tom Burton's house so I could pay for the damage. His dad had hired us to clean up the backyard.

Tom was waiting for me in front. He was all excited about something. "Check it out. Dad bought a chipper. He told me we could use it if we're careful."

I followed him around to the backyard. At first, I didn't even notice the thing. It was painted green and it was rusted in spots, so it sort of blended in with the background. But as I got closer, I could smell oil and gasoline.

"That's a chipper?" I asked. It didn't seem like much. There was a gas engine at the bottom, along with some gears and belts. Above that, there was just a metal box with a chute coming out of the top. The whole thing sat on wheels so it could be rolled around easily.

"Yeah. That's it. Here." Tom handed me a pair of safety glasses. He put on a pair himself. Then he leaned over and yanked the starter cord. The chipper sputtered and roared. Then the roar dropped down to a loud, steady purr.

"Watch this. It's awesome," Tom said. He grabbed a branch from the ground and put one end into the chute on the chipper.

I couldn't help jumping away. The chipper snatched the branch out of Tom's hand. But it didn't swallow its victim quietly. It made the most awful shrieking, grinding, screaming sound. A flurry of wood chips sprayed out the other end.

"Cool, huh?" he said, turning toward me and grinning.

Something about seeing that branch sucked inside the chipper and reduced to tiny bits of wood made me feel like my own spine had been ripped out and fed into the chute. *Get a grip*, I told myself. This was just a machine. It was a machine whose scream scraped all the way down my nerves and through my gut, but it was still nothing more than a machine.

"So," Tom said, "we can take turns gathering and chipping. Okay?"

"Yeah. I'll start gathering." I moved across to the other side of the yard, as far away from the chipper as I could get. I piled sticks in the wheelbarrow until it was full and brought the load over to Tom.

Every time the chipper ate another branch, I flinched. No matter how far away I was, I couldn't help it. After an hour, Tom said, "Hey, want to switch? I shouldn't have all the fun."

"Not yet. I like picking up the sticks." That was a lie. My back was sore from all the bending and lifting, and my shirt was soaked clear through with sweat. But I'd happily pick up a million more sticks before I'd go close enough to feed that chipper.

"Fine with me," Tom said.

After another hour and two more offers to trade places, he started getting suspicious. "Come on, let's switch," he said when I was dumping a load of sticks next to him.

"No, really, that's okay. You're having fun with it. I don't need a turn."

Tom stared at me for a moment, then asked, "You scared?"

I shook my head. "Nope."

He reached down and grabbed a stick. "Here. Prove it."

"I don't have to prove anything." I wondered if it was worth arguing about. Things could go either way. If I stood up to Tom and he backed down, everything would be fine. But it could also become a problem. If Tom pushed, I wasn't sure what I would do. Maybe I'd put one stick in the stupid thing. Or maybe I'd just walk away. Rather than wait to see what he was going to do, I went to gather more sticks.

I hadn't gone more than ten feet when I heard the scream. I dropped the handles of the wheelbarrow and spun around. "It's got me!" Tom was screaming and trying to pull his hand from the chipper.

I ran toward him, reaching out to try to drag him free. I knew it. I knew the machine was dangerous.

"Got ya," Tom said. Laughing, he stepped away from the chipper and held up his hand, wriggling all five fingers.

"That's not funny," I said. I froze, one hand on his elbow, the other grabbing the edge of the chipper's chute. I jerked my hand back and saw that I'd sliced my finger on a rough edge of metal. It wasn't a bad cut, but I'd left a splash of blood on the chipper.

"You should have seen your face," Tom said.

"And you shouldn't have stuck your arm in there," I said. I reached to wipe the blood off the machine but stopped. I didn't want to touch it again.

"I just pretended to stick my arm in." He paused and stared at me. "Hey, you really are scared of it, aren't you?"

"I'm not scared. I just don't like it. Okay?"

Tom grinned. "Sure. No problem."

As I turned away from the chipper, the strangest thought crossed my mind. *It had tasted my blood.* Behind me, I could almost sense it wanting to chase after me for another taste.

Tom went back to feeding the chipper. Finally, around three o'clock, he suggested we knock off for the day. That was fine with me—I was exhausted.

I headed home and plunked down in front of the television for a while. I was too tired to move or think. After dinner, I went to bed.

The crunch of tires on the road disturbed my sleep. The shriek of the chipper woke me.

I sat up, startled. But there was silence in the night.

Maybe I'd dreamed it. I walked to the window and

looked out toward the street. My hand clenched the windowsill when I realized there was a form in the darkness that didn't belong. Something dull and heavy sat in the front yard.

Tom's playing a joke. That had to be it. He'd wheeled the chipper over from his house. Well, he'd gone to a lot of work for nothing, I thought as I got back in bed. I wasn't going to say anything about it. I'd pretend I'd never heard it.

In the morning, I looked out the window as soon as I got up. There was nothing in front. I checked the backyard, too, and saw nothing out of place, except for the things that were normally out of place. The usual messy assortment of stuff I'd forgotten to pick up was spread around the yard. The old swing set and sandbox that Dad had built when I was little were still there. But that was all.

At breakfast, nobody mentioned hearing any strange sounds. "Ever use a chipper?" I asked Dad. Maybe I was hoping the question would jog his memory.

"Nope," he said, "but I'd sure like to."

No, you wouldn't, I thought as I finished my cereal.

"I'll bet you slept well last night," Tom said when I reached his house.

"Like a log," I said. I knew what he was trying to do. He wanted me to tell him I'd been awakened by the chipper. But I wasn't going to play along.

"Let's take a break from the sticks and start on the weeds," Tom suggested.

I didn't have any problem with that. The work was just as hard, but at least it didn't involve the chipper. By the end of the afternoon, we had pretty much cleaned out all of the wild growth.

I went to sleep early again. And I was awakened again by a shriek. The chipper was in the middle of the lawn, tearing the night with a cry like it was shredding giant branches of hardwood. The shriek almost seemed to be calling my name.

"No," I said, walking away from the window. I refused to believe it was there. I went back to bed and put the pillow over my head, muffling the sound. I still heard it, but now it was only a whisper.

The chipper wasn't on my lawn in the morning. Something else caught my eye—a small pile of wood chips. Right next to the pile was an impression in the grass. The rake. I'd left the rake out last weekend. I remembered walking past it a couple of times. I kept forgetting to put it away.

I didn't want to go back to Tom's place. If this was his idea of a joke, I wanted nothing to do with him. If he wasn't pulling some kind of joke—then I really didn't want to go over there. But I had to get the money.

Tom wasn't outside when I reached his house, so I knocked on the door.

"Tom isn't here," his mother said. "There's been an accident."

My mind filled with the image of Tom being swallowed

by the chipper. I shut my eyes, but the picture didn't go away. After a moment, I realized his mother was still talking.

"It's nothing serious, but he has to stay in the hospital for a couple of days."

Nothing serious? "Uh, what did you say happened?" I hadn't heard that part.

"He slipped on the basement steps and broke his ankle," his mother said. "Maybe you can go visit him later. But I'd really appreciate it if you could finish the cleanup today. Do you think you could do that for me? We've decided to sell that chipper. Once the cleanup is done, we really don't have much use for it."

"Sure," I blurted out before I could stop myself. I went into the back to gather the last of the sticks. The whole time I worked, I didn't turn my back on the chipper. It sat in the corner of the yard, silent, as if waiting and planning. There was no way I was going to feed it. I took the sticks to the far side of the yard and shoved them under the bushes.

"That's it. I'm done," I said to myself as I hid the last load. "Leave me alone," I said, looking at the chipper.

I got my money, then went home.

That night, it didn't wake me. I was already awake when I heard it rolling down the road.

I looked out the window. The chipper didn't stop in the yard. It went to the porch. I heard a thunk as it bumped against the front steps.

It couldn't get in. The steps were too high.

As I looked out the window, the chipper rolled around the house toward the backyard.

There were no steps by the back door. The chipper could smash right into the house.

I had to stop it.

I raced out to the yard and grabbed the first thing I could find. It was a baseball bat.

As the chipper came around the side of the house, I swung at it with all my strength. Big mistake. It felt like I'd hit a concrete wall. My hands went numb.

The chipper rolled toward me.

I took a step back.

The bat started jerking in my hands as if someone was pulling at it. I tried to hold on—but it was yanked from my fingers. It flew into the chute of the chipper and turned to sawdust before I could even scream.

All around me, stuff was flying from the ground, getting sucked into the chipper. The same force tugged at me. It took all my strength to move away. I stumbled over something and fell backward.

Soft dampness broke my fall. I clutched at the sand in the sandbox, grabbing a double handful. The chipper loomed over me. I stood, still fighting the force that tried to pull me into the chute.

I couldn't hold back. My hands got sucked into the chute. I let go of the sand. I could feel air from the whirring blades blast across my fingers as I fell forward. There was an ear-ripping scream. The chipper jolted to a stop as the sand fouled the gears. It jerked twice more, then fell quiet.

I stepped back and grabbed more sand to pour down the chute. Then I gathered pebbles and small stones and tossed them in the hopper. It was over. "Eat that, you piece of scrap." I brushed my hands and walked away.

My sleep wasn't disturbed again that night.

In the morning, I looked out into the yard. There was no sign of the chipper. I imagined it crawling off, like a dying animal. It didn't matter where it had gone. Those awful blades would never spin again. I checked the clock. It was after ten. I'd slept late.

I went out to make sure everything was all right. As I walked around to the front of the house, Dad called me from the garage.

"Look at this," he said. "I bought it this morning from Mr. Burton. It needed a lot of work, but I think I got it fixed. Darn thing had sand in it. Can you believe that?"

I took a step back. Dad braced one hand on the edge of the chute and grabbed the cord with the other. "Yes sir-ree," he said, "once you get the blades spinning, this baby will chew up anything."

I tried to shout, but my throat closed tight and all that came out was a thin gasp.

Dad pulled the cord.

The chipper roared to life.

That freed my scream. But the engine drowned out my cry. I felt myself being pulled forward. Dad gripped the edge of the chute harder, as if fighting for balance.

The chipper sputtered and died.

"It's bad," I told him. "It's a bad machine."

Dad shrugged. "I wouldn't say that. It still needs some work. But don't worry. I'll get it running as good as new. And then we'll have some fun."

"Get rid of it," I said.

Dad ignored me and looked at his finger. "Hey, I cut myself. Well, no big deal." He grabbed a wrench and went back to work, humming happily as he fixed the chipper.

I turned and ran. But it didn't matter. I had nowhere to go, and nowhere that I went would be far enough to escape the chipper.

MUG SHOTS

A hike seemed like a great idea to Vince and his friends. The first hour was fun as they followed the trail through the woods of Great Bear State Park. The second hour was okay. The third hour, when they noticed they weren't on the trail, wasn't a whole lot of fun.

"We're walking in circles," Vince said. He stopped and stared at a tree that looked distressingly familiar.

"No we're not." Keaton shrugged off his backpack and let it fall to the ground.

Bill and Sherman didn't say anything. They just dropped their backpacks, too.

"We need to pick a direction and go straight until we reach a road," Vince said. He remembered reading something about following a stream when you're lost, because running water usually led to where people were. But they hadn't seen a stream, a river, or a creek. Not even a pond. Vince didn't want to think too much about water. He'd emptied the last drop from his canteen an hour ago, and his mouth was so dry he was afraid his tongue would crack.

"Which direction?" Keaton asked.

Vince shrugged. "I don't know. But we need to do something. Let's just pick a direction." He pointed past the tree. Nobody argued, so he started walking.

The other guys sighed and picked their packs up.

An hour later, they spotted the cabin, half-hidden in a cluster of spruce trees. "Maybe someone's home," Vince said. He went up to the small porch and knocked on the door.

There was no answer. Vince tried the knob. It didn't turn.

"We need to get in," Keaton said. "They might have a phone."

"In the woods?" Vince asked. "Yeah, right."

"Maybe they have water," Sherman said.

"We definitely need to get in," Keaton said. He walked around the side of the cabin.

Vince followed him. They tried all of the windows, but they wouldn't move.

"We gotta break in," Keaton said when they got back to the porch. He kicked the door. It didn't open. He kicked it harder. Something cracked. He gave it a third kick, and it swung open.

"There's a kitchen over here," Keaton called as he dashed inside. "I found a sink."

Vince and the others ran to the sink. There were a dozen mugs hanging from pegs on the wall. Vince scanned them. They all looked pretty silly. One had a picture of a bear on it. Another had a rabbit. There was a snake, a crow, and a fish. They'd been hand painted. Vince spotted a blank mug and grabbed that. By then, the other guys had already filled their mugs from the sink and were chugging down water so fast it was sloshing over their chins and running down their shirts. Vince noticed Keaton's mug had a rabbit on it. Bill had a snake and Sherman had a bear.

As they crowded around the sink, Vince joined them, drinking two full mugs of water before he stopped. "I've never been so thirsty."

Feeling better, he put his mug down on the kitchen table, filled his canteen, and looked around. "No phone," he said. "We'd better get out of here." He felt bad about breaking the door, even though it was Keaton who'd done it. But they'd needed water.

As he turned to walk out, Sherman groaned.

"You okay?" Vince asked.

Sherman groaned again. Except it was a weird groan—more like a growl. He put his mug down on the counter.

The next groan was definitely a growl. Sherman held his arms out. Dark fur was sprouting from them. His nails grew into claws. His nose pushed out into a snout, filled with large teeth.

Vince backed away. Keaton backed away. Bill froze.

Sherman turned toward Bill and took a swipe at him. Bill ducked just in time. Sherman's paw struck the bear mug, sending it flying into the wall. It shattered.

Sherman groaned.

It was a human groan this time—not the growl of a bear. "I don't feel good," he said. He staggered out of the cabin.

Vince felt like he'd just been punched in the head. But he gathered his wits and looked at the other two mugs. Keaton had drunk from a rabbit and Bill from a snake. Keaton's mug was on the counter. Bill's was still in his hand.

As scales formed on Bill's arms, he threw the mug to the floor, shattering it. Then he staggered outside.

Vince watched as Keaton turned into a large, stupid-looking rabbit. "Talk about a perfect choice," Vince said. The rabbit sniffed and twitched, then tried to get up to the counter where the mug was.

Vince figured he could help Keaton out, but he wanted to take a moment to enjoy the sight of the pathetically helpless rabbit. After sniffing around for a while, Keaton used his head to push a chair toward the counter, ramming it a little bit at a time. It took him a couple minutes to move it close enough. He managed to hop up on the chair. From there, he got up on the counter. Using his head again, he pushed the mug off the edge, so it fell to the floor and shattered.

As soon as Keaton turned back into himself, he dashed for the door.

"Hey, wait for me," Vince called. "Come on, I was going to help you if you really needed it."

Annoyed at the others for leaving him, Vince took another look at the mug, just to reassure himself that there wasn't an animal on it. *Glad I didn't drink from the fish,* he thought. That wouldn't have been pretty.

He saw nothing on the mug. No animal. Nothing.

He glanced at his arm. And saw nothing.

Vince held up both hands in front of his face. Nothing. He'd become nothing.

He reached out to smash the mug. His hand went right through it.

He kicked the table.

Nothing.

"Guys! Come back. You need to smash my mug," he shouted.

The three guys walked back into the cottage.

"Thank goodness." Vince enjoyed the feeling of relief that washed over him.

"Nope," Keaton said. "I don't see him here."

"Break the mug!" Vince called.

Bill nodded. "Yeah. I guess he ran out."

"Guys . . . ?"

"Yeah, he's gone. Nothing could hide in here," Sherman picked up the blank mug, looked at both sides, then shrugged and put it back down.

The three of them turned and walked out. Vince followed them, shouting and screaming, but they heard nothing.

FORGOTTEN MONSTERS

Things grow dull in the Hall of Forgotten Monsters. I can tell that I am close to fading completely away. Nobody believes in me and, even worse, nobody fears me anymore. There was a time—ah, what a time it was—when the very thought of me sent shivers of terror down the spines of even the bravest children.

We are a sad and miserable group, here in the Hall of Forgotten Monsters. Across the way, I can see the Stegalith. What a fine creation he was, unstoppable, crushing everything beneath his terrible stone body. How folks must have trembled at the thought of him. And the Dracae, huddled together in that corner. There was a time when mothers could make their children behave by scaring them with tales of the Dracae.

No more.

We are forgotten. We are unfeared.

There must be a way to return. Once, every child knew of me. It was I who rode the moonlight through their closed windows and carried them away if their minds held even one thought of me. The name of the Wander-ban was whispered from child to child. "Don't think about him," they warned. "If you think about him when he's near, he'll get you. He'll snatch you right from your bed. It's best to never think his name."

That was me. Those were the glory times.

They said I had a thousand heads, each with a thousand teeth.

This is true.

They said those I stole suffered a lifetime of terror during each instant I held them in my grasp.

This, too, is true.

They have forgotten me. My place has been taken by other terrors—the vampire and the zombie, the mummy, the boogeyman. But I have a plan.

There is a way to return.

It might not seem possible. I know that the Stegalith and the Dracae would say it can't be done. No one has ever returned once belief began to fade.

But I have a plan.

I will find a teller of tales. I will search for one whose mind I can enter. I will slip my story into his mind and have him tell it to the world. Then they will fear me and I will no longer fade. I will grow strong again.

I have found the one. He is ready. It is easy. I am in his mind. I will begin with words that will draw the reader into the tale. He is used to ideas coming to him from out of nowhere. He will not question this gift—he will just tell my story. And the children will read about the Wanderban. They will whisper my name and fear me, and I will be real again. I know the perfect words. I have been thinking of them for many centuries. I will whisper the words now, and he will write them: "Things grow dull in the Hall of Forgotten Monsters. I can tell that I am close to fading completely away."

Good. He is writing the story. Soon, you will read it. Fear me. Think of me. Whisper my name. I will return.

A WORD OR TWO ABOUT THESE STORIES

Every writer gets asked, "Where do you get your ideas?" As with the first two collections, I'll end things here by answering that question.

Mr. HooHaa!

A lot of people feel that clowns are scary. I was thinking about this one day and decided to explore the issue. I guess I could have come up with some sort of story about why clowns are scary, but the idea that hit me was "what if they are even scarier under their makeup?" As you'll see in these notes, one of my main tools is asking "what if" questions.

You Are What You Eat

Back when I was in high school, someone I knew told me he'd tried baby food. He claimed he'd done this just out of curiosity, but I suspect some sort of dare might have been involved. That incident bubbled up into my mind a while back, and I figured it would make a good scene with which to start a story. Memories make a good launching pad for stories. The nice thing is that you don't have to stick with what really happened.

Spin

I think this is one of my favorite stories in the collection. I try to start each writing day by jotting down a "what if" question. Most of these questions lie around for weeks or months before they get used. But one day, I wrote: "What if you could make sand spin?" The idea instantly grabbed me, and I wrote the first draft of the story that same day.

The Tunnel of Terror

I was at Knoebels Grove, a very cool amusement park in Pennsylvania with a great classic coaster, when I saw an old funhouse ride. (It was in much better shape than the ride I describe in the story.) That led me to think about whether it is worse to go through a scary ride with your eyes open or shut. And that thought, of course, led me to this story.

A Nice Clean Place

I started out with the idea that pigeons were some sort of cleaning device (yup, another entry from the "what if" files). The rest grew from that. I guess there's a bit of a message here, too. But that's not my main goal. The people who litter aren't going to stop what they're doing because they read a story.

Tied Up

If you aren't a baseball fan, a game can seem endless. If you are a fan, you might wish a game went on forever. If you're a writer, you might just get interested in setting a story in an endless game. In this case, I stepped up to the plate with nothing in mind other than an endless game.

Predators

There's been a lot in the news recently about the dangers of chat rooms and other online places. When I hear about any kind of danger, I like to think of a way to twist the threat into a story.

The Curse of the Campfire Weenies

I'd originally planned for the title story to be about bike weenies. (You know who they are—those far-too-serious riders with their funny shorts and high-tech helmets.) But then my editor, Susan Chang, suggested campfire weenies. I loved that idea. Thinking about campfires made me think about people who like to tell scary stories and about people who think they are experts but really aren't.

Cat Napped

My cats catch stuff once in a while. They're very proud about this. It wasn't a big leap in my mind to go from mice to leprechauns. (You can get lots of good story ideas by taking something ordinary and changing just one small part of it.) I started out with the opening scene and let the story go where it wanted. Had I been in a different mood, I guess it could have ended badly for the leprechaun.

The Unforgiving Tree

This began as a title. (An interesting title can inspire a whole story. Usually, the title leads to some sort of "how" or "what if" thought.) *The Giving Tree* is a picture book by Shel Silverstein. Some people love that book. Others hate it. Ask your favorite librarian to explain this to you. My mind twisted the title, and I knew I had to write a story to match. How could a tree be unforgiving? The answers are endless.

Bobbing for Dummies

I just started out with a couple kids trashing a party. It was interesting seeing how bad they could be. I didn't like the story all that much when I first wrote it, because the ending seemed too disconnected with the rest of it. Then I got the idea to add the "make a wish" part with the kid in the turkey costume. That's why revision is my favorite part of writing.

Eat a Bug

I was thinking about loneliness and friendship when this idea showed up. Why are some kids so popular while others don't have any friends? Instead of writing about the lowest outcast on the playground, I though it would be interesting to start with someone just above that level. I had no idea it would lead me in such a tasty direction.

Throwaways

Yet another tale that sprang from a "what if" question. This is probably my most absurd story. Sadly, kids do get tossed out in various ways. I think what makes this story work is the contrast between the strangeness of what is happening and the matter-of-fact voice of the narrator. He takes everything in stride.

Touch the Bottom

If you've ever fished on a lake, you know that the depth can vary a lot from point to point. It's fun to imagine that a spot is bottomless. I think most kids enjoy seeing how far, how deep, or how fast they can go. This story was an attempt to see where that drive would lead.

The Genie of the Necklace

I thought it would be interesting to let a girl discover a genie and be able to get whatever she wanted. I knew right off that if she was a nice girl who was generous to her friends it wouldn't be that interesting a story.

Alexander Watches a Play

I got this from my "what if" file. The basic concept was, "What if a kid went to a movie and saw himself in it?" The fun part, for me, is finding a way to bring the "what if" to life. I switched the idea from a movie to a play and made the main concept a bit weirder than a kid just seeing himself in it.

Mrs. Barunki
I had this idea in the back of my mind for a long time. I've always been fascinated by the thought of someone teaching misinformation. For example, imagine a pair of parents who speak nothing except Latin around their kid. Just think what his first day of school would be like.

Murgopana
This story hit me when I was thinking about linguistics. Languages are pretty fascinating. Some of them have structures that are very different from English. There are many languages that, like the one in the story, change a noun by adding a prefix or suffix. (If someone tells you to put down this silly book, let that person know you're learning about linguistics. That will silence most critics.)

Eat Your Veggies
Life seems to be overflowing with rules. I love to take a rule and think about what will happen if someone breaks it. Unfortunately for my characters, whatever happens usually isn't very pleasant.

Inquire Within
Even though this isn't a Halloween story, I'm not surprised at all that it popped into my mind right around the

end of October. That, after all, is when you can count on seeing some lighthearted segments about witches on the news. I was watching one when I started thinking about witch hunts, which led me, first of all, to the idea for the ending.

Three

When I first became a parent, I promised myself I'd never do any of that typical parent stuff like counting to three. That promise didn't last long. (Being a parent is a whole lot harder than it looks.) But, to be honest, I had no idea what I'd do if I ever reached three. And, to tell the truth, I still don't know.

Fat Face

This is one of those rare cases where I started off with a character. I wanted to write about a kid who was taunted for being overweight. I was a fat kid in elementary school, so it wasn't hard to dream up a suitable opening scene, though nothing as extreme as that ever happened to me.

The Soda Fountain

I've written some stories based on unpleasant childhood memories (most notably, "A Little Off the Top," from *In the Land of the Lawn Weenies*, which grew from my dislike of visiting the barber when I was little). This one started with a pleasant memory—getting a fresh-mixed soda at a soda fountain. I had no idea what would happen after

Ben walked through that door. But as I wrote the opening scenes, the idea came to me.

Sniffles
I was thinking about the term "allergy shot," and I realized it could have more than one meaning. This is another nice way to get ideas. There are all sorts of words and phrases that can be given fun meanings. I'm sure you can think up lots of examples that are just as interesting as "allergy shot."

Sidewalk Chalk
This actually happened to me. Okay—not the dinosaur part. But I did pick up a piece of sidewalk chalk in my garage and try to figure out what it was. When I started writing this story, I had no idea where it would go. Maybe I was influenced by the fact that I don't draw very well.

Don't Ever Let It Touch the Ground
Another rule. Maybe this book should have been called *Attack of the Rule Weenies*. Just about every rule and superstition kids hear can be the source of a story. Hmmm, maybe there will be some rule weenies down the road (as long as they don't step on a crack while they're on that road).

Picking Up
As any parent (or kid) can tell you, the messy room is always an issue. While I can't solve the problem in real life, I can at least fix things in fiction.

Head of the Class

Many years ago, my daughter had a teacher who would hold up students' bad tests and tell everyone their grades. She once ripped a kid's paper to pieces in front of the class. I felt that someone like this deserved a nasty fate—at least, in fiction. So I started writing a scene with an unpleasant teacher, fully intending for her to meet a ghastly end. But, as you can see, I lost control of the plot and had to abandon my original intentions. That's fine. I kind of like how it came out. And I can always take another shot at vengeance down the road.

Halfway Home

There really is a use for a philosophy degree. I like thinking about paradoxes, dilemmas, and fallacies. Here's a classic one to get you thinking: "This statement is false." Think about it. If it's false, it has to be true. But if it's true, it must be false. "Halfway Home" is inspired by Zeno's paradox, which takes several forms. For example, no matter how fast you run, you can never catch someone who has a head start, because you first have to make up half the distance, and then half of what remains, and so on. I'll stop, now, or this entry will never finish.

Hop to It

I think I was watching some kids play with grasshoppers when this idea jumped into my mind. Or maybe I was the one making the grasshopper jump. If so, I swear I never squished it. As I look back over my story collections, I can see that insects seem to provide me with an endless source of ideas.

Nothing Like a Hammock

I have a hammock. And I love to watch spiders. All I needed to do was combine the two things. This is usually a great way to get an idea. (If you look at a building and see a giant robot, you're on your way to a story.) The nice thing about combinations is that there are so many of them. If you take fifty different things, you can produce 2,450 unique combinations.

Puncturation

My daughter waited until eighth grade to get her ears pierced. That got me thinking about the whole process. I started out just having someone go in for a piercing, without knowing what would happen. For the record, I have nothing pierced. Yet.

The Chipper

One of the scariest stories I've ever read is Stephen King's "The Mangler." He wrote it about a laundry machine that scared him. The first time I saw a chipper, I had the same kind of reaction, so I figured it would be interesting to put it in a scary story. I actually did use a chipper once, but it was a teeny-tiny electric one. No way I'm going near the real thing.

Mug Shots

Okay, this is going to start sounding tedious, but this one also came from my "what if" file. In this case, I originally just thought about kids turning into animals. The twist popped into my mind right after I started writing the opening. There are countless ways I could have gone. Feel free to come up with your own version of the ending.

Forgotten Monsters

I have no idea where this idea came from. It just sort of popped into my head, as if someone whispered it in my ear. Weird.

READER'S GUIDE

ABOUT THIS GUIDE

The information, activities, and discussion questions that follow are intended to enhance your reading of *The Curse of the Campfire Weenies*. Please feel free to adapt these materials to suit your needs and interests.

WRITING AND RESEARCH ACTIVITIES

I. **What Makes a Story Scary?**

A. Examine the stories in *The Curse of the Campfire Weenies*, looking for ways in which these "warped and creepy tales" turn the ordinary on its ear. Then write a two- or three-paragraph answer to the question, "What makes a story scary?"

B. Go to the library or online to create a bibliography of great scary-story authors and their books, from *Frankenstein* author Mary Shelley to R. L. Stine of *Goosebumps* fame. Invite classmates or friends to read and summarize some of the stories from your list. Compile the information into a class "Scary Story Reading List," complete with book titles, authors, plot summaries, and fun illustrations or graphics.

c. Does everybody like a good scare? Create a class survey about whether kids enjoy scary books or movies, have a favorite scary tale, know of a creepy place, or like to play spooky games. Can they sleep the night after watching a scary movie? Have they ever reconsidered an activity after hearing something scary about it? Compile the results of your survey on an informative poster, including illustrations and a chart or table.

II. Warped Writing Prompts

A. What happens if you take a cliché like "You Are What You Eat" to its literal extreme or explore its double meaning? Go to the library or online to find a list of proverbs and aphorisms by the great American Benjamin Franklin, including "Little strokes fell great oaks," and "The cat in gloves catches no mice." Use a creepy interpretation of a Franklin quotation as the basis for a warped tale.

B. Examine the way selfishness, laziness, and greed on the part of protagonists or others result in terrible outcomes in some tales. Try to remember the details of a time when you misbehaved or broke a rule. Jot down as many details as you can recall, such as who was present, where the event took place, what you did, and what you thought. Then write the creepy chronicle of a fictional character who acts as you did in your memory then gets what he or she "deserves!"

c. Like Zeno's paradox that leaves one character eternally "Halfway Home," mathematical and scientific principles can make great story starters. Visit the renowned Smithsonian Institution online at www.si.edu and spend at least five minutes exploring one or more "Science & Technology" feature or exhibit. Write a sentence describing the most interesting, thought-provoking, or creepy fact you discovered to use as the basis for a short, scary legend.

III. What If . . . ?

A. Reread the afterword, "A Word or Two About These Stories." Write a short essay explaining why you think David Lubar chose to include this information along with his stories, and what inspirations or insights you found most interesting.

B. One of Lubar's favorite story starters is to ponder "What if . . . ?". With friends or classmates, discuss the value of this thought process. Is it a good way to start a story—especially a scary one? Make a brainstorm list of "What If's" of your own.

c. Despite his long career as a video-game programmer, David Lubar does not feature scary video-game tales in this anthology. Write a list of at least five video-game related "What If . . . ?" story prompts to inspire writers. Trade prompts with friends or classmates and try writing the stories. Compile the efforts into a class anthology entitled *The Vengeance of the Video Weenies*.

QUESTIONS FOR DISCUSSION

1. What does the opening sentence of the first story tell you about its narrator? Are you the kind of reader who can "stare a werewolf in the face and laugh"? How does the opening paragraph make you reflect upon your own identity as someone who has chosen to read a scary-story collection?

2. Do you agree with the narrator of "Mr. Hoohaa!", who suspects it's better to have a reason to be afraid of things than to have an unreasonable fear? Why or why not? Do you think this story collection is about reasonable and unreasonable fears? Explain your answer.

3. Scary stories often involve ordinary situations viewed from an extraordinary, scary point of view. Reread the opening paragraphs of several stories to find the moment at which the normal becomes bizarre. (For example, the reference to the "ninety-seventh inning" in the opening line of "Tied Up.") Describe a real-life experience of your own where something commonplace turned strange. Would it make for a good scary story? Why or why not?

4. "You Are What You Eat" takes a common cliché to its absurd—and terrifying—extreme. What other stories in this collection bring a familiar expression to an extreme dimension? What might the author be trying to say about the power of language through such stories?

5. Explore the author's use of food imagery, from the collection's title to the serene experience of "The Soda Fountain" to the candy bar in "Fat Face." What other stories play with notions of food and eating (or being eaten)? What are some important connections between food and being a kid?

6. In "Bobbing for Dummies," "The Genie of the Necklace," and "Inquire Within," characters act in selfish or unkind ways. Do these characters' unkind acts result in their unpleasant fates? Would nicer characters have survived the same situations? What other stories explore this notion? Is the author suggesting that it is a good idea to be a nice, well-behaved kid?

7. From "Eat a Bug" to "Hop to It," bugs are a recurring image in the collection. Are bugs powerful? Why do humans feel vulnerable to these small creatures? What other stories involve or make reference to bugs? How does the author use the image of bugs to explore themes of large-versus-small in the world?

8. How are the power of knowledge and wrong-headed learning explored differently in "Mrs. Barunki" and "Head of the Class"? How do these notions play out in other stories in the collection? How can you be sure of what you know?

9. With what types of extraordinary powers does the author endow ordinary objects in "Sidewalk Chalk,"

"Mug Shots," and other stories? Do you have a penny, rabbit's foot, or other object that you consider lucky or magical? Describe the object and the role it plays in your life. Is this rational?

10. "Predators" and "Cat Napped" surprise readers by reversing the perceived victims and villains. How are such reversals used in other stories in the collection? How is reversal an important literary device used throughout the book?

11. How do kids' relationships with their parents play out in "Three" and "*Murgopana*"? Compare and contrast your attitudes toward your parents or guardians with the attitudes of the kids in stories from the collection.

12. Which stories in this book feature themes of destruction? Who are the destroyers in these tales? Which stories feature themes of desperation—of characters trapped in some sort of endless night or unsolvable riddle—and who are the desperate individuals? What conclusions might these tales lead you to draw about the author's perspective on the power and plight of kids?

13. Are you scared of clowns? Of vampires or scary carnival rides? If you were going to write a story for this collection, what scary image, event, or character would you feature and why?

14. Is "Forgotten Monsters" the scariest story in the collection, or the least frightening? Why? How does this story make you reflect on yourself and your power as

a reader of stories? How do "Mr Hoohaa!" and "Forgotten Monsters" create a logical frame for the rest of the stories in the collection?

15. What do you think are the most important themes or ideas that are carried through many stories in this collection? How do the book's final tale and epilogue expand it from a scary-story collection to an exploration of words, writing, imagination, and the idea of reality?